D0965491

ALSO BY SARA SAEDI

Never Ever

Americanized: Rebel Without a Green Card

THE LOST KIDS

Sara Saedi

VIKING

VIKING
An imprint of Penguin Random House LLC
375 Hudson Street
New York, New York 10014

First published in the United States of America by Viking,
an imprint of Penguin Random House LLC, 2018

LIBRARY OF CONGRESS CATALOGING-IN-PUBLICATION DATA IS AVAILABLE
ISBN 9780451475770

Printed in U.S.A.   Set in Fournier   Book design by Kate Renner

1   3   5   7   9   10   8   6   4   2

For Bryon & Ellis
Thank you for keeping me young

prologue

"phinn, are you listening? Where's Wylie Dalton?"

Dead.

Sleeping at the bottom of the ocean.

Permanently trapped in the folds of my mind.

Tucked away in a corner of my heart.

All of the above.

"You have a chance to do the right thing here. Answer the question."

A fan buzzed overhead. The steady beeping of the heart monitor made Phinn insane. He missed the *pop-pop* of *parvaz* flowers and the whirr of carefree teenagers flying above him. He missed the melodies of the island. Hell, he missed blue sky.

"Where's Wylie Dalton?"

That question had haunted Phinn from the moment he'd heard Wylie plummet into the ocean, and now it was being asked with the urgency of someone looking for a set of missing keys. All he wanted was to see Wylie again, to hold her, and to tell her that the moment he'd met her, he'd given up on making her part of his intricate revenge plot.

Phinn's plan had always been to befriend Joshua. The son in trouble with the law seemed the most vulnerable among the Dalton siblings. But there Wylie had been on the dance floor, surrounded by friends yet somehow creating the illusion that she was alone. From where Phinn had sat that night, he'd barely been able to make out the emerald shade of her irises, but he'd seen a trace of pain behind her eyes. On that rooftop in Brooklyn, he'd forgotten about her dad and the reasons he'd engineered a run-in with the Dalton kids. Their future didn't feel premeditated anymore. It felt inevitable.

"If I knew where she was, don't you think I would have found her?" Phinn finally responded.

"What did you do to her?"

I lied to her. I broke her heart. I held her captive.

"Nothing. I didn't do anything to her. I want to go home."

"I'm afraid that's not going to happen."

Phinn did the math. He'd been here for ten days. That meant two hundred and eighty-five more days to spare before he'd turn eighteen.

"How old were you when your parents died?"

"What do you have on that little clipboard?" Phinn asked. "A list of every upsetting question you could ask me?"

"This will go a lot more easily if you cooperate."

"Five. I was five when my parents died."

"And how did they die?"

The same way Tinka's and Maz's and Gregory's parents had died. At the time, he'd thought it was just an elaborate game of hide and seek; that, when he found them, they were only pretending to be asleep. He'd yanked his mother's hair, screaming at her to wake up. He'd scraped her skin with his fingernails as Lola's mother had pulled him away.

Phinn looked into the eyes of his interrogator and waited until he was certain he wouldn't cry:

"They killed themselves."

sleepless nights

the water was still for once. Lying on the floorboards of the boat, Wylie almost felt like she was back on dry land. After three weeks trapped on this vessel, she was getting used to the cold dankness. The surrounding abyss of ocean no longer left her overwhelmed. The days of motion sickness slowly retreated into the past. Despite all she had grown accustomed to, the sleepless nights continued to torture her, and tonight was no exception. It didn't matter that every joint and limb was weak from hours of exercise— Wylie's mind refused to slow down. She spent every night searching for constellations and counting stars, but nothing seemed to lull her to sleep.

It had been twenty-one days since she'd last seen her brothers. The Daltons had never spent that much time apart. Here, on this boat, she had no parents and no siblings. She was an orphan. The lost kids were her only family now. She sat up and looked at the sleeping bodies, sprawled in every direction. Charlotte snored loudly next to her like she did most nights. Wylie tried to shut out thoughts of smothering her with a blanket. It wasn't Charlotte's fault she could fall asleep anywhere she laid her head down.

"I love sleeping," Charlotte explained to her. "Every night that we go to bed, we wake up one day closer to taking the island back. One day closer to going home."

Home. Wylie wasn't sure where that was anymore. She hoped it was still her cozy bungalow, but how could she live on Minor Island without her brothers? By nightfall tomorrow, she and the lost kids would sail to the patch of land that had changed the course of her life, and everyone seemed certain Micah and Joshua would be there when they arrived.

"They couldn't have gotten away," Hopper told her. "They'd never steal a boat in time, and they couldn't fly all the way back to the mainland."

But Wylie had learned that nothing was guaranteed. Maybe her brothers had made it back to their Manhattan brownstone. For all she knew, they were sitting on the fire escape together right now, wondering if they'd ever see their sister again. If she closed her eyes long enough, she could make believe she was back in her old bed, wrapped in worn out flannel sheets. What she would give to wake up in the morning and brush her teeth in a normal sink and take a hot shower in an actual bathtub!

The snores were even louder now. Wylie gently tapped Charlotte's shoulder.

"Charlotte," she whispered. "You're snoring."

Charlotte groaned and turned on her side. The rumbling

subsided for a few minutes until it started back up again. After three weeks of insomnia, Wylie wasn't sure what tormented her more: sleep deprivation or Phinn.

She'd finally conquered it last night as she'd let her mind drift to the party at Vanessa's and remembered what it had felt like to see Phinn across the rooftop. She'd recalled how everyone else melted away except for them. Before the memories could turn dark, before she could remind herself that Phinn was a monster, she'd fallen asleep. But tonight, the very thought of him made her restless mind even more alert.

Wylie stretched out her legs and quietly pulled herself up to her feet. She grabbed the thin blanket that barely kept her warm and wrapped it around her shoulders. She'd perfected the art of moving without disturbing others in their sleep. Her feet knew every floorboard to avoid and every sleeping body to step over in the pitch dark. All she had to do was follow the soft sounds of guitar strumming to the bow of the boat.

"Couldn't sleep again?" Hopper asked, as she tiptoed toward his regular spot.

"Nope."

"What about last night? You were sleeping like a baby."

"Charlotte must've been snoring less."

"No way. I bet they could hear her all the way on the island."

"Mind if I hang out here for a while?" Wylie asked, lying down before he answered.

"Not in the slightest."

Hopper wasn't always this nice to her. During her first

few days on the boat, he'd mostly ignored her or given one-word responses to every question she'd asked him. And he'd never asked any questions in return. *He'd be terrible on a date*, Wylie had thought.

"He doesn't like most humans," Lola explained at the time. "Don't waste your time trying to win him over."

Perhaps it was boredom that made Wylie determined to be his friend—or maybe she needed a challenge. After their daily training sessions on the boat, the lost kids spent the rest of the day fishing and perfecting their weapons. Most of them filled the hours rehashing every bad thing Phinn had done to them. But time had given them more distance than it had given Wylie. For her, conversations about Phinn were still a painful reminder of her own mistakes. So she turned her attention to Hopper. It was like her secret game: *Person who doesn't like most humans, I will make you like me.*

It wasn't an easy pastime. In the beginning, Wylie's sarcastic quips and witty jokes had gone over like an atheist at a bible study. Hopper would respond with a blank stare, mutter an excuse under his breath, and walk off to another corner of the boat. *Try to find something you have in common*, Wylie told herself. Their mutual hatred of Phinn seemed like an obvious starting point, but Wylie preferred to avoid the topic of her ex. She tried to bond over music by casually referencing the classic rock albums her dad used to play for her growing up, but Hopper shut down even more at the mention of her parents. When Wylie tried a more forward approach and asked if she could pass the evenings with him while he played guitar, Hopper said he'd rather be alone.

Finally, Wylie remembered his manifesto. There was no e-mail or texting on this boat, but Hopper himself had admitted he communicated best on paper. So Wylie wrote her own manifesto. She told her story, in her own words, and confessed how stupid she felt about falling for Phinn.

She folded the sheet of paper into a rectangle and slipped it under the strings of Hopper's guitar. He never mentioned reading it, but the following day, he meandered next to her as she tried in vain to fish for her dinner. They both knew she never caught anything.

"If you can't sleep tonight, you can come hang out with me." He said it casually, as though the ocean hadn't shifted from the invitation.

Now, every night since, she snuck over to his corner of the boat and listened to him clumsily play guitar. Hopper was a proud lefty, which meant he normally used his right hand to press down on the frets. But, thanks to Tinka, he was now missing three fingers on that hand and had to fumble with his left hand along the fretboard. The chord changes were still slow and unsteady, but Wylie hummed along to distract him when he got frustrated.

"Maybe she has a deviated septum," Wylie said.

"Who?" Hopper asked.

"Charlotte, obviously. What if we pinned her down, plied her with vodka, and did surgery to fix the thing? You hold her arms and I'll go in with a knife."

Hopper's face broke into a smile at the suggestion. It felt like such a victory when Wylie could get him to break from his usual scowl.

"You're such a weirdo, Dalton," Hopper said.

"A weirdo you're stuck on a boat with, Hops."

"I know. I should have left you on that rock."

Wylie playfully tugged on his long curls. She hadn't expected to get used to his appearance. Phinn was chiseled and clean cut, but Hopper was neither of those things, though it was hard to know what his face looked like under his beard. If she saw him in her old life in New York, she'd think he was a homeless person. Most days, he smelled like one, too, but so did she. Good hygiene wasn't really an option on a small boat filled with over a dozen sweaty kids.

"I would give anything to go to sleep," Wylie replied.

"How about when we get back to the island tomorrow, after we do the whole, you know, overthrowing Phinn bit, we'll go to the Forbidden Side, and pick a bunch of *rahat* flowers and sleep for days."

Wylie felt like an imposter whenever Hopper talked about Minor Island. He always made references to plants or landmarks she wasn't familiar with, but she hadn't lived there nearly as long as he had. She felt like one of those people who called themselves New Yorkers after spending only a year in the city.

"No one ever told me about *rahat* flowers," Wylie admitted.

"Good. I like getting to be the one to tell you about stuff. They're red, almost burgundy. They're twice as big as *parvaz*, but they don't make any sound when they grow. Phinn never liked people taking them. But they made me feel . . . invincible. Aldo and Patrick gave them to me to help with anxiety, but if you take enough, they make you sleep for hours."

Wylie remembered spying the plant he was describing through the bars of her cage, just out of reach. Lola had mentioned there were herbs that were native to the Forbidden Side, but she'd never mentioned *rahat* flowers. Wylie wondered what else about the island she had yet to discover.

"They sound tropic."

"Tropic?" Hopper teased. "I don't know what that means. I don't speak Phinnish."

"Whatever. I could have used a few *rahat* flowers when Phinn had me locked up," Wylie said.

"I used to beg him for them, especially after they chopped off my fingers, but he wouldn't allow it."

"Well, he won't get a say now."

Their plans, or what the lost kids referred to as Operation Exile, fell squarely on her shoulders. They had grown accustomed to calling Wylie their secret weapon. But none of them knew she had a knack for disappointing the people who counted on her most. She didn't have the heart to tell them she might lose her nerve. They talked about how they'd get rid of the cages on the Forbidden Side. Hopper promised he would personally nail down the floorboards to the panic room and would never make anyone hide in the dark. The girls would no longer be herded into the clinic, forced to take birth control. Everyone could use their preferred form of contraception.

"Condoms are kind of a drag, though, you know," Hopper joked.

"It's a good thing no one in their right mind would have sex with you. Especially not Nadia," Wylie replied.

Hopper had confessed that he'd developed a crush on Nadia when he lived on the island, and Wylie loved teasing him about it.

"Not looking like this, she won't," Hopper agreed.

He dug a pouch out of his guitar case, opened it, and handed Wylie a razor and a pair of scissors.

"When Phinn let me out of my cage and shipped me away, this is more or less what I looked like. If I don't want some crazy Phinn loyalist to bash my head in when we get to the island, it'll probably help if I don't look like myself," Hopper said. "Will you do the honors?"

"Are you sure? I had some bald Barbie dolls as a kid because I tried to give them haircuts."

"I'll take the risk."

The dull blades of the scissors made it tough to slice through Hopper's dense curls. Wylie cut them an inch from his head. She tried her best to keep the trims even, but she had no experience with cutting hair.

"Do you think Phinn will put up a fight?" Wylie asked, squeezing the blades of the scissors together.

"If he's as stubborn as he used to be, yes. But when news spreads about what he did to Lola . . . he won't have much choice but to go to the mainland."

✦ ✦ ✦ ✦ ✦ ✦ ✦

WYLIE WONDERED WHAT PHINN WOULD DO IF HE was forced to live in New York. He had no family in the city. He had no formal education. She pictured him wandering around the streets, wielding no power and no influence. Eventually, he'd find some poor sucker to take him in, but he'd never get over being shunned from his home. *No one will love him in New York*, Wylie thought to herself. She felt a pang of sympathy.

"All done," Wylie announced.

Hopper ran his fingers through his short curls. His beard was now longer than his hair. He eyed the razor on the ground next to them.

"Can I trust you with my beard, or will you accidentally slice my neck open?"

"As long as you don't breathe or move, I promise not to draw blood."

Hopper stroked his beard, not quite ready to part with it. Wylie knew that, though he would never admit it, it was his security blanket. Hiding his face allowed him to disguise the fact that he had feelings.

"Maybe I should keep the beard for now," he said.

"No." Wylie was adamant. Even with a haircut, the beard would make him recognizable to an army of kids who wanted him dead.

She used the scissors to trim his facial hair. Once it was short enough, she poured water over his cheeks and jaw line. As tufts of hair disappeared from his face, Wylie noticed high cheekbones, meandering freckles, and full lips that had been impossible to make out all this time. The angles of his face were more defined than she'd expected. She thought he'd look younger or boyish without his usual scruff, but he looked even more like an adult now. If he worked on his conversational skills, he might just have a chance of stealing Nadia away from Patrick.

"How old are you?" It suddenly occurred to her to ask. She wasn't sure.

"Seventeen. Same age as you," he answered.

Phinn had said the same thing to her when they met. It had been a half-truth, but so was most everything else he'd said that night.

"I was sixteen when Phinn recruited me to the island."

Wylie used the bottom of her T-shirt to dry off Hopper's face. He let his fingers graze over his cheeks.

"You survived. I didn't slice your neck open."

"And for that I am grateful."

They didn't have to say it out loud to know what the other was thinking. Tonight was their last night on the boat. Tomorrow, they could die or end up in cages on the Forbidden Side again. Or, they could start over on the island. With any luck, Wylie and Lola would be whipping up a hearty breakfast for the kids. Between bites, Micah and Joshua would talk about how much they'd missed their sister's cooking. Phinn would be halfway to the mainland. Slowly, Wylie could put the pieces of her heart back together again and forget that a certain boy ever existed.

"Now what?" Hopper asked.

Wylie picked up his guitar and handed it to him.

"Play me something."

Hopper strummed a few chords. Wylie curled up on the chilly planks of wood, closed her eyes, and listened to the melody slowly forming beneath his hands. Hopper said the guitar was out of tune, but Wylie didn't know the difference. The thoughts in her mind slowly swirled, and the rooftop in Brooklyn came into view.

Don't think about Phinn, she told herself as she saw his face and drifted into sleep.

operation exile

the boat was moving too fast. Wylie wanted to yell at Hopper to slow down, but he had no control over the wind speed. The sun was about to retire for the day, but they still had several hours before they were close enough to stake out the island. She tried to conjure up the moment it would reveal itself in all its glory. She imagined the palm trees swaying forward in the wind, almost bowing at them in welcome, as they ventured through the trail. She wondered if the fireflies would help light their path, and if the tempo of *parvaz* flowers would go from languid to allegro, to announce their presence. But even joyous thoughts of the island did nothing to calm Wylie's nerves. With every sudden movement of the boat, she could feel her breath quicken and her limbs tremble. *Don't let them see you like this,* she told herself as she slipped off into the cabin of the boat and locked herself inside the shoebox-sized bathroom. She would only allow herself to hyperventilate in private.

Breathe in, 1-2-3. Breathe out, 1-2-3.

If it worked for Micah, then it should work for her, too. She thought back to the night her parents announced they were getting divorced and how Micah had barged into her bedroom gasping for air.

"I think I'm dying!" he told Wylie, frantic.

"You're not dying. You're having a panic attack," Wylie had told him.

She walked Micah back to his room and got him to lie down on his bed. She told him to inhale and exhale deeply. His heart rate gradually returned to normal, and his eyes fluttered as he fell asleep. She stayed by his side until she was certain he was in a deep slumber, and then she collected the half-empty bottle of bourbon from his nightstand and dumped the remainder of the booze into the sink.

Breathe in, 1-2-3. Breathe out, 1-2-3.

Wylie wasn't dying now. Her heart wasn't going to stop. She was just having a panic attack. She tried to battle her anxiety by closing her eyes and repeating the words from Hopper's manifesto over and over again in her head.

I'm going to exact revenge on my captor. I'm going to take away everything that means anything to him. I'm going to take his land and put him behind bars and do everything to him that he did to me.

A knock on the door interrupted her fifth go-round.

"Who is it?" Wylie managed to ask.

"It's me, Lola. Are you okay in there?"

She wanted to tell Lola that she was never coming out of the bathroom. That she would prefer to go on living out the rest of her life in here if it meant avoiding Phinn.

"Just a minute." Wylie splashed water on her face from a bucket and took one last deep breath, as she opened the door. Lola looked at her and frowned.

"You look like crap," she said.

"That's good, right? Phinn's never gonna buy my story if I look like I've been yachting for the last month," she replied, trying to smile through the panic.

"What's going on with you?" Lola asked.

There weren't many places for privacy on the vessel, but the rest of the lost kids were currently sharpening their spears and practicing their drills. Wylie stepped out of the bathroom and sat down on a pile of blankets. She looked up at Lola, her hands still shaking.

"I can't do this," she admitted.

"Can't do what, exactly?"

Protect my friends. Seduce Phinn. Occupy the island. Wylie hated herself right now. She wanted to be brave. She wanted to be like Lola. She wanted to be the kind of girl who could charge her way through the Clearing with a spear in one hand and a torch in the other. She wanted to be like the heroines in the books she loved to read. The ones who didn't fear death and never doubted themselves.

It suddenly felt wrong to fake her confidence. At least this way, if everything went awry, she could say that she'd rung the alarm and given Lola fair warning. It wasn't too late to come up with a contingency plan.

"I'm sorry," Wylie said, verging on tears. "You picked the wrong girl. I'm a mess. I'm a screw-up. I will ruin this for all of you."

"No, you won't." Lola placed an arm around her. "You're

the strongest person I know. You got away from Phinn. You swam for your life in the pitch-black ocean. You're a survivor, just like the rest of us."

"I'm going to get you killed. You're all going to die because of me, and I'll never be able to forgive myself," Wylie cried.

"Let's get some air," Lola suggested.

The temperature had dropped on the deck. Wylie's teeth clanked together as she tried to listen to Lola's pep talk, but at least the wind and sprays of mist from the ocean helped slow down her breathing. They'd spent every day of the past three weeks going over their plan. Wylie and Hopper would be the first to enter the island. They'd go through the trail together, and part ways briefly as Wylie scoped out the Clearing to make sure everyone, even the insomniacs, had retired to bed. And that's when she'd make her way to Phinn's bungalow and pretend she had gone through hell to make her way back to him. He'd be so distracted by their happy reunion that he wouldn't hear Hopper enter the room to restrain him. The rest of the kids would divide and conquer. They would split up into groups of three to take over the clinic, the dining room, and the Forbidden Side. The three locations were vital to life on the island. If they cut off access to food, medicine, and the prison camp, then the locals would have to fall in line. Lola would go to Maz's room to recruit him to their side. Wylie had argued against the Maz portion of the plan. She didn't like the idea of her friend roaming the island alone, but Lola reminded her that if anyone could get Maz to turn against Phinn, it was his girlfriend of two decades.

"Remember the day we met?" Lola asked

Wylie nodded. How could she ever forget it? Lola was the only person she'd ever seen look graceful while gutting a fish.

"I had so much kitchen envy," Wylie recalled. "You were nice, but you didn't want to have much to do with me."

Lola laughed. "I knew from the moment I saw you that we would be friends, and you would change my life . . . in a good way."

"I *ruined* your life."

If Wylie had never moved to Minor Island, then Lola wouldn't have discovered the secret about Wylie's dad. Lola wouldn't have confronted Phinn and been left for dead in the middle of the ocean.

"You helped me see Phinn's true colors. You helped me see that we'd been bowing down to someone we didn't need to bow down to. Before I met you, I didn't believe we could live without Phinn. But now, with your help, we're going to take the island back from him. The best days are ahead of us, Wylie. And that's why you have to stop doubting yourself."

"Why?"

"Because," Lola said, "you're my best friend, and you're the only one I trust with my life."

There was no guarantee that Wylie wouldn't screw it up, but Lola had suffered enough because of her. This was the only way she knew to make up for the pain she'd caused.

As the boat picked up speed, they distracted each other by talking about the chickens and how much they missed them. They agreed they would throw themselves an epic homecoming party, and they would find someone else to cook the food.

"You'll get to see your brothers again," Lola said.

"I will," Wylie agreed.

In a matter of hours, she'd be standing in front of Phinn. And regardless of how much he beamed at the sight of her, and regardless of how many apologies he made, she would not deviate from the script. She would not, under any circumstances, tell him she was the bait and he was the hostage.

* * * * * * *

EMOTIONS WERE HIGH AT THE SIGHT OF THE ISLAND, but nobody could scream at the top of their lungs the way they wanted to. They couldn't make any noise at all. All Phinn's boats were parked in their usual spots. Unless Phinn had found a way to fly to the mainland, he was most likely sleeping in his bungalow right now.

"Are we ready?" Lola asked.

Wylie was the first to nod her head.

Hopper carefully steered the boat toward the deck as the rest of them got their weapons ready, in case they met any unexpected visitors. They were on high alert as Hopper stepped off the boat and tied it to a wooden pole. He gave Wylie the thumbs-up signal, and she quietly stepped onto the deck and jumped into the water. If Phinn was going to believe that she had swam back to shore, she had to be soaking wet. She pulled herself back onto the deck and waved good-bye to the group.

"Be careful, Wylie," Lola said, as she pulled her into a hug.

"I will."

The walk along the trail filled Wylie with dread. Hopper and Wylie knew better than to risk speaking to each other, so she silently tolerated her terror. Even the slightest noise had potential to wake up the entire island and destroy weeks of careful planning. Wylie was scared that if she breathed too loud or coughed or sneezed, they'd find themselves surrounded. Every step either of them took seemed to be amplified with the island so eerily quiet. *This is a good sign*, she thought. *No one's awake in the Clearing. Everyone's asleep by now. They'll never know what hit them.*

Hopper didn't seem nearly as terrified. The only time Wylie noticed him falter was when they walked past the Forbidden Side. Overgrown ivy covered the fence and obscured the graffiti that had supposedly been Hopper's calling card, created by Phinn to keep everyone afraid of him.

After a few more yards, they arrived at the point in their journey where Wylie would have to enter the Clearing by herself. Hopper gave her an encouraging nod, and Wylie resisted the temptations to hug him or run all the way back to the boat. Instead, she kept walking. She heard none of the music or partying she had witnessed the first time she'd seen the Clearing. She picked up a jar to catch fireflies, and though the source of light was weak, she was surprised to see the lagoon covered in leaves and debris. Beneath her feet, she heard the crackling of dead sugar root. The memorial they'd erected for the lost kids was scattered in pieces all over the ground. And there were no lights or movement coming from any of the bungalows. Something was very wrong.

Wylie headed back down the trail and found Hopper swinging his spear in the air.

"It's too quiet," Wylie told him. "And the Clearing's a mess. It must be some sort of diversion. Maybe they're hiding. I think they're waiting for us. Someone tipped them off."

"No one could've tipped them off. Let's go to Phinn's bungalow."

But as they made their way past the Clearing and up their stairs toward the row of bungalows, Hopper knew Wylie was right. Aside from rustling leaves and the now inconsistent *pop-pop* of *parvaz* flowers, there were no other sounds they would have expected to hear on a populated island. Broken doors and lost possessions lined their path as they walked past the huts and noticed that each one was empty. When they arrived at Phinn's bungalow, they discovered the hinges on the door were broken. They slowly entered, but there was no sign of him. His bed was damp from a leaky roof, and the floor was crawling with roaches and spiders—insects Wylie had never seen before on the island. His closet and drawers had also been ransacked. Hopper placed his brittle hand on her shoulder. Wylie wasn't sure if he was trying to comfort her or keep himself steady.

"Don't say it," Wylie begged.

"There's no one here," Hopper said. "There's no one on this island."

Three weeks earlier

"wylie!" Phinn screamed as he kicked and flailed in the sky. His eyeballs were on fire. But with his vision temporarily impaired by the pepper spray, his hearing seemed to improve. He could make out the sound of water splashing below as Wylie swam away from him.

"You'll drown out there, Wylie! Swim back to the island!"

As the splashes below receded, he had no idea if she could hear him anymore. Maybe she was swimming back to shore. He tried to open his eyes, but the cool air made them sting even more. This was not how their love story was supposed to end. They were supposed to live happily ever after together. Phinn had planned to tell Wylie the truth about her dad in his own way, in his own time. He knew she'd be upset. He'd promised he'd never lie to her again. But he was certain she'd never dream of going home and giving up a life free of responsibility. Besides, her father had hurt her probably worse than he'd ever hurt Phinn. Gregory left Wylie's mom for another woman. It was his decision to break up their family. Phinn had merely taken Wylie away from the dysfunction.

"Wylie! You're going to get yourself killed!"

The burning in his eyes was slowly beginning to subside. His body dropped a few feet as the effects of *parvaz* tapered off. Phinn never hated his parents as much as he hated them right now. Couldn't they have at least taught him how to swim before they took their own lives? Couldn't they have taught him *something*? It was their fault that he couldn't dive into the ocean and swim after Wylie. It was their fault that he was scared to death of the water.

Phinn opened his eyes again, and this time, it didn't feel like tiny needles were pricking his irises. But all he could see was the vast darkness of waves below. There was no sign of Wylie. He turned his body toward the beach, and screamed for help, but no one could hear him. He moved his arms and legs as quickly as he could to fly back to solid ground but kept dipping closer to the current.

"Wylie, please!" he yelled again. "I need your help! I'm going to drown if I fall in!"

After their parents died, Lola's family had warned them there were crocodiles in the ocean. For years, he believed them, but as he got older, he realized it was just a tall tale to keep the kids out of the water. If the orphans they were stuck raising believed there were monsters in the sea, then they would never go in the water and drown. And now, if they were watching somewhere from the heavens, Lola's family would probably be happy to see him sink. He was, after all, the person who'd stolen the island from them.

He thought he'd plummet quickly into the water, but the *parvaz* took its time wearing off completely. Inch by inch, he moved closer to a certain death. Phinn tried to float on his back the way Wylie had taught him, but the current was violent. His head bobbed above the surface, but the tide pulled him farther away from land.

Don't fight it, he told himself. Even if there were no witnesses, he could still choose to die gracefully. Why live if the only person he'd truly loved wanted nothing to do with him? Phinn had hurt a lot of people in his lifetime, but he'd never been more disgusted with himself than the day Wylie confronted him in the Clearing and screamed at him that she was merely a revenge plot against her dad.

"Never hold grudges," Lola's mother had warned him when she and the rest of Lola's family left the island. "It'll poison you." At the time, it seemed like empty advice from the people who would rather leave their home than coexist with him.

Phinn relaxed his body and let the waves carry him to the end of his life. He wanted to think of Wylie and the handful of happy moments they'd shared together, before she learned he was completely unworthy of her. But none of those memories came into view. Phinn's life wasn't flashing before his eyes; his *mistakes* were. The day he'd seduced Tinka when he knew full well his best friend was in love with her. The vulnerable and naïve kids he'd plucked from the mainland for his own amusement. Every sad and desperate face that begged for mercy from inside his cages on the Forbidden Side. The horror and confusion in Lola's eyes when she realized that Phinn was going to sail off without her. And lastly, Wylie's look of sheer hatred just before she showered his face with pepper spray.

I deserve to die, Phinn told himself.

A blinding light broke through the surface of the water. *"Phinn. . . ."*

The voice was crisp and clear. Wylie was here with him.

"Wylie!" he responded, but it came out garbled.

He felt a pair of arms wrap around his waist. Phinn looked behind him and saw Wylie's face, smiling at him in a way that reminded him of the day he built her a basketball court.

"You're safe now," she whispered in his ear.

"I knew you'd come back for me," Phinn said, but he wasn't sure she understood him through the distorted sounds of salt water.

Wylie maneuvered her body to face him, and that's when he noticed she had fins where her legs used to be. She was naked from the waist up, but her long brown hair covered her chest.

"There are no crocodiles in the ocean, silly," Lola had teased him when they were kids. "Only mermaids."

+ + + + + +

PHINN COUGHED, HALF-EXPECTING A STREAM OF water and a school of fish to pour out of his mouth. His face felt raw and hot from what he hoped was just a sunburn.

Grains of sand had made it into his nostrils and eyelashes. He opened his eyes, but all he could see was pale blue sky. The last thing he remembered was hallucinating, as he sunk in the ocean.

"Of course the bastard didn't die."

He knew the voice better than he knew his own.

Tinka's face came into view, staring at him from above. Years ago, they had gone to the *parvaz* field and climbed the willow tree together. They'd agreed they wouldn't do it under the influence of magical flowers, and would rely on their strength to get to the top. But Phinn had miscalculated the sturdiness of a branch, and had plummeted to the ground as it snapped under his weight. When he'd opened his eyes, Tinka's face flooded with relief. It was the happiest he'd ever seen her: that moment when she'd discovered he was still alive. The girl staring at him now looked disappointed. Phinn broke eye contact and noticed that the entire population of the island surrounded him. No one looked relieved to find him alive. He scanned their faces, hoping to spot Wylie among them, but she was nowhere to be found.

"We need to get him to the clinic. We have to take his vitals," Patrick said, his face inching into Phinn's line of sight.

"Not until he takes us to his bungalow," Bandit said.

Something had shifted during the night. Did they find out what he did to Lola? He looked more closely at the faces of his friends, hoping he could get a better read of their expressions. Micah and Joshua glared at him from the front lines. So they hadn't escaped, but no one had thought to put them in handcuffs. Bailey fidgeted and let her eyes travel over anything other than Phinn. Patrick ignored Bandit's demand and placed a stethoscope against Phinn's chest, but Aldo didn't bother coming to his aid. Maz was the only one with an expression of sympathy on his face. Or maybe it was pity. It was hard to tell.

"I'm sorry," he mouthed, but Phinn was too afraid to ask what he was apologizing for.

"I told them your secret, Phinn," Tinka said. "I told them about the war room where you keep your secret files on everyone. I'm done protecting you. Now everyone else can know what an elder you are. Get up. Take us there right now."

Phinn quickly pulled himself to a seated position and scooted his body away from the mass of concerned citizens.

"No," he said. "Not until we find Wylie."

"Our sister's gone." Joshua's voice fell an octave when he said it. "We've looked everywhere for her . . . except your secret bungalow."

* * * * * * *

"FOLLOW THE LEADER, PHINNY."

He could still hear his mom's voice in his head sometimes, though he wasn't sure anymore if that was really what she sounded like. But he did have a distinct memory of standing in the Clearing with Tinka and Gregory and Maz when they were little. Their parents stood in a line in front of them and taught them how to play Follow the Leader. Even then, Phinn preferred to do all of the leading and none of the following.

"He's going to run his own company someday," his father had joked.

"His own company?" his mother said. "Our Phinny's gonna run the world."

Phinn remembered shaking his hips side to side and giggling as he watched Tinka, Maz, and Gregory do the same. He remembered that afternoon he didn't miss any of his toys they'd left back home, and that he was content sleeping on piles of leaves, and that even though food was scarce, he could almost ignore the fact that he was hungry. His parents were with him, and they were laughing, and they didn't yet need to eat a handful of red flowers to make themselves happy.

Now he wanted to stop the march through the jungle. He wanted so badly to be a child again and go back to that moment. He wanted to turn to the fifty kids that were following him in single-file and tell them to shake their hips or rub their bellies and pat the top of their heads. Instead, he forged ahead, determined to atone for his sins.

"It's not too late to turn around," Maz advised him under his breath. "Or if you've got any matches, I'll set the place on fire before anyone gets a chance to walk in." Maz and Tinka were the only people Phinn had ever taken to the war room.

Phinn shook his head. "That won't be necessary."

He could have come up with a million reasons to ignore Tinka's demands to bring the kids here, but he was exhausted from lying and making excuses. And part of him hoped if he made amends for every terrible thing he'd done, the universe would somehow reward him with Wylie.

They reached the end of the trail where the trees and coarse layers of ivy came together to obscure the bungalow. Phinn borrowed a knife from Maz and hacked into the vines, creating a small enough crevice for them to squeeze through one by one.

"This is tropic," Elliot said as soon as he feasted his eyes on the structure. Phinn couldn't help but smile at the compliment. Elliot was an expert architect, and Phinn was proud he'd created something that met his approval.

"Why'd you keep this from us?" Bandit asked.

Because it would end our friendship, Phinn wanted to say. Bandit had only lived here for two years, but he'd quickly become Phinn's favorite recruit. He was smart and considerate and usually brimming with joy. He never took the island for granted and loved it nearly as much as Phinn did. And that was why Phinn had invited him to be a member of the inner circle, even though he'd known him a fraction of the time he'd known everyone else. Phinn trusted him completely.

"I needed a place to . . . conduct business," Phinn replied.

The kids watched as Phinn pressed his body against the logs and a door opened. The last time Phinn had visited the bungalow was hours before prom, when he'd carefully removed several bundles of dynamite to set off the explosion on the beach. He'd purchased it the same day he'd kidnapped the Daltons from New York, not quite sure when he'd use it. A potential recruit had taught him how to construct a makeshift timer so the dynamite could explode without anyone being there to ignite it. Phinn couldn't remember the kid's name anymore, but he'd been put off by his passion for explosives, and decided not to invite him to the island.

The war room was far too small a space to fit everyone, so people crowded around the entrance, trying to peer in. With everyone watching, Phinn broke open the floorboards and took out the box of files he'd hidden underneath them. He handed the kids every file he had on them, including the less incriminating ones he kept in locked drawers.

It was Bailey who let out the first guttural scream.

"My mom died!" she cried. "She died ten years ago. . . ."

Bailey's mother had been sick with breast cancer for three years before she lost her battle. Maz had learned about it on a trip to the mainland, and he'd thought they should offer Bailey an opportunity to return home and say good-bye. But Phinn refused. If they let one person go back to the mainland for a family emergency, then they'd have to let *everyone* go back whenever they pleased. Within a year, the whole world would learn about Minor Island, and someone would have successfully invaded. Besides, everyone had agreed to renounce their old lives when they stayed here.

The files included information about sick or deceased relatives, but they also came with Phinn's psychoanalysis of each desired recruit, and the ways he could manipulate them into following him to the island. The information was for his eyes only, so he'd never been careful or eloquent with his word choice. Terms like "pitiful," "naïve," and "feeble" showed up in several files. He remembered in Bandit's, he'd scribbled: *So unloved and unwanted that he'd follow me to hell if I asked him to.*

Bandit's paperwork documented his mother's struggle

with drug addiction, including the months she spent sober after child protective services had taken him in as a ward of the state. Days before Bandit was supposed to be released back into his mother's custody, she'd fallen off the wagon. What Bandit didn't know until now was that Phinn had caused his mother's relapse. He'd found someone to slip her *rahat* flowers, and when Bandit was told he'd have to remain in foster care, he ran away and slept on the streets. Shortly thereafter, Bandit agreed to leave everything to come with Phinn to the island.

"You gave my mom drugs!" Bandit confronted Phinn as he shoved him against the wall of the cabin. Phinn felt like his spine might become dislodged, but he found the damage to his body comforting. He deserved it. He would have liked Bandit to beat him to a bloody pulp, but Maz yanked him off.

Some of the kids had been more easily convinced to follow Phinn on his boat, and he hadn't needed to topple any chess pieces in their lives to recruit them. But the files didn't just evoke despair for what Phinn had *done* to his followers—they were just as upset by the secrets he'd kept from them. How could he casually suggest Bailey name her band the Youth Brigade when he knew her mother was dying? How could he make jokes with Nadia during a fitting when he knew that her little brother had tried to commit suicide on the anniversary of the date she'd gone missing? How could he badmouth Elliot's parents for kicking him out of the house for being gay without telling him they'd become gay rights advocates after the disappearance of their son?

There was guilt and regret and plenty of remorse and

self-hatred, but none of his feelings mattered to anyone. He tried his best to keep his own tears at bay while mumbling apologies.

Now you know the real me, he wanted to say. *Now you know I'm not a good person. Now I can stop pretending.*

Between the threats and the punches and the spit hitting his face, Phinn looked around for Tinka. He expected to find her laughing or applauding as she watched the charade unfold, but her expression was grim and solemn. She'd asked for Hopper's file, and was sitting on the ground with it still unopened on her lap.

Joshua kept a safe distance from him throughout the ordeal. Phinn wanted to check on him, but he kept getting ambushed along the way. Of all the recruits he'd invited to the island, Joshua had been the most skeptical and the hardest to convince to stay. If memory served him correctly, the file stated that "chief of staff" was merely a vanity title to appease Wylie's brother. And though that had been true at the beginning, it stopped being the case only days into the job.

Micah didn't share his file with Joshua, but Phinn knew its contents were far more upsetting. It was nearly sixteen years ago when Phinn's curiosity got the best of him, and he sought out Gregory in New York City. Before then, he'd been too angry to look up his old friend and see what had become of him, though he'd heard through various sources he'd been living with Olivia Weckler and her wealthy family. Phinn had exiled Olivia after she'd taken a sabbatical in the states and returned past her eighteenth birthday. Over time, he'd realized she was aging and forced her to leave the island. A few years ago, Patrick and Aldo had returned from the mainland with news that Olivia had gotten her medical degree and started her own pharmaceutical company.

"She's specializing in anti-aging medications," they revealed to Phinn, and they'd all laughed at the irony.

Gregory's career path, however, had nothing to do with his past on the island. He'd made a name for himself in finance and had earned enough money to buy a brownstone in a fancy neighborhood in Manhattan. Sixteen years ago, Phinn had sat on a stoop across the street from the Upper East Side dwelling and watched it for hours. He was almost hypnotized by it. What was it like to live in a house? He didn't remember. What was it like to be an adult and have children? The sheer thought of it made his stomach turn.

Eventually, a woman stepped out with one hand to her stomach. She skipped down the stairs in a hurry and hailed a cab. Even with the cold and faraway look in her eyes, Phinn could tell she was strikingly beautiful. She had to be Gregory's wife. He quickly flagged down a cab and followed her. The taxi dropped the woman off in front of a medical clinic. Phinn's cab idled by the curb, and he watched as she paid the driver and clumsily got out of the vehicle. She was so focused on the contents of her purse that she hadn't noticed Gregory standing outside of the clinic. Phinn rolled his window down and slid low in his seat. They were yelling, so it was easy to hear every word of their argument.

"You were just going to get rid of it without even telling me?" Gregory yelled.

"We didn't plan for this," the woman argued. "I never

wanted kids in the first place. I definitely never wanted *three*."

"Maura, how could you say that?"

The mixture of anger and desperation in Gregory's voice revealed how much he cherished his children, and that he considered it a blessing to have more. Phinn could play a long game. He could wait until Gregory's kids were teenagers, and then he would take them away from their father.

Eventually, Gregory and Maura stopped fighting and left in a cab together. A year later, Phinn visited the brownstone again, and saw a tired Maura walk down the stoop with an infant tucked into a Babybjörn. Until today, only Gregory, Maura, and Phinn knew just how close Micah Dalton had been to never existing. But now that Micah had sifted through his file, he knew the truth. His mother hadn't wanted him. Phinn knew the feeling.

"I can't live here with Phinn." It was Bandit who made the declaration. "Either he leaves the island, or I leave."

"Bandit, please . . ." Phinn started to beg. He couldn't let Bandit return to the mainland. The United States weren't safe for a black kid from Brooklyn.

"No!" Bandit cut him off. "If Phinn doesn't get exiled, then I'm getting on a boat and leaving. I'd rather get old than stay here with him."

Phinn could still hear the hurt and fury in Wylie's voice when she had told him she would rather die young than grow old with him. The other kids echoed Bandit's sentiment. No one wanted to live with Phinn. In one day, he'd gone from their leader to the resident pariah.

"Don't send me away," Phinn blurted. "Please. Lock me up in a cage on the Forbidden Side and keep me there forever, but please don't send me away." He knew he sounded hopeless and terrified, but he didn't care about looking strong anymore.

"Lock you up?" Bandit asked. "Like you did to Grace and Charlotte and Jersey and the other kids? You want *us* to stoop to *your* level?"

Phinn could feel himself getting frustrated now. They were all complicit in what had happened to the lost kids. Bandit had been a prison guard for months. He could have easily used a key to set each one of the lost kids free, but he never did.

"It's not a harsh enough sentence," Aldo spoke up. "If we lock him up, he'll stay young. If we really want to punish Phinn, we need to make it permanent. He needs to go back to the mainland and grow *old*."

Most of the kids agreed with Bandit and wanted Phinn to leave the island immediately. For once, Tinka remained silent. Maz stepped in to put a stop to the protest.

"That's enough," he said. "No more bullying or rash decisions. I think we should take the subject of Phinn's exile to a vote."

Dozens of hands shot up in the air.

"Not now. We're acting on emotion. We'll have two weeks to consider Phinn's fate. Each of you will cast an anonymous ballot, and we'll count the results publicly. If the majority of you call for Phinn to leave, then Bandit and I will personally take him to the mainland and drop him off."

No one argued with Maz, and Phinn didn't put up a fight. It was a fair solution, and he would accept his fate. But if there was a God or anyone watching over him, then he hoped Wylie would make it back to the island before the day they sent him away for good.

toy soldier

the fourteen-day grace period felt like a death sentence. Only a handful of locals had been exiled back to the States. Phinn had never been liberal with the punishment because he knew the more people he shuttled back to New York, the sooner the whole world would know about the island. But those decisions had been abrupt and without much warning. There had been no time for the person being exiled to say their good-byes or count the hours and the minutes before they were forced to leave Minor Island. Some thought it was cruel to make them depart so suddenly, but Phinn was now certain it was humane. It was so much worse to make a person wait out the days in mourning. How was Phinn expected to say good-bye to the *parvaz* field he'd worked so hard to nurture and grow? How could he leave behind the cascading waters of the lagoon that allowed him to cool off without any fear that he could drown? Worst of all, how could he walk away from feeding the chickens and watering the herbs and vegetables? He'd spent the bulk of his free time over last two weeks in the garden making sure the plants thrived in Wylie's absence, and he didn't want his hard work to go to waste. He made Maz promise to find someone who could remember that the apple flowers needed more sunlight than water, but that the woodmeg and chipney dried out if they weren't properly doused twice a day.

"It needs to be someone who's good at taking care of things. Someone with a nurturing side," Phinn recommended. "Talk to Joshua. See if he'll do it."

"You don't have to worry. We'll take good care of the garden," Maz promised. "When Lola comes back, she'll have my head on a plate if everything she planted is dead."

Phinn wondered if he should tell him that Lola was never coming back. But he had already taken away Maz's girlfriend; he couldn't take away his hope, too. Over the last few days, whenever he heard Lola's name, it reminded Phinn that getting sent away was a fair punishment. He was lucky they weren't executing him.

"And anyway," said Maz, "The vote hasn't happened yet. You might be surprised. Even if no one will admit it, we need you here."

Maz had always been an optimist, but Phinn knew better. By tomorrow morning, he would be on a boat headed to the mainland. He'd packed his belongings, including the cash he'd stowed away in case he was forced to spend an extended period of time off the island. He would take a small pouch of *parvaz* flowers with him. They'd only last a couple of weeks anyway, so it didn't make sense to smuggle more than what he needed. And lastly, he made sure to keep his good luck charm in his shirt pocket and right next to his heart. The tiny mirror strung on the chain that had belonged to his mother would somehow keep him safe, he convinced himself. Especially since Wylie had worn it.

Every night, he flew around the perimeter of the shore and landed in the Clearing to roast sugar roots and listen to the hum of the wind bristling through the palm trees. When he was ready to sleep, he'd tiptoe over to the Forbidden Side, careful not to get trapped in quicksand. He plucked the *rahat* flowers and threw them in a pouch.

His last morning on the island, he woke up in Wylie's bed. He ripped a piece of paper from Lola's journal, wrote a long letter, and slipped it under Wylie's pillow. He took Lola's journal and slipped it into his knapsack. If he left it behind, someone would eventually find it, and it would only confirm that they'd done the right thing by freeing themselves of Phinn. He hoped they would eventually regret sending him away.

At least he knew the garden would miss his presence, so he spent his remaining hours among the plants that had grown and flourished under his care. What would he even do on the mainland? He had no purpose. He had no family left that he knew of. Years ago, he'd learned that his mom's sister lived in Connecticut, but he couldn't exactly show up at her doorstep. What would he say?

Hi, Aunt Barbara. It's your nephew, Phinn. Yeah, the same one who was born more than fifty years ago.

During meal times, Phinn avoided the dining room. He couldn't suffer through the humiliation of no one speaking to him or looking at him. So he ate his berries and oatmeal alone in the garden and talked to the chickens.

"Hey, don't be so sad," he told them now. "You guys will survive just fine without me. I'm leaving you in good hands until Wylie comes back. You'll meet your new keeper today. He's a bit Type A, but that's good. He won't let a single meal fall through the cracks."

By the time he took his last bite of breakfast, the French doors from the kitchen swung open, and Joshua walked in with a notebook in hand.

"Hey," he said.

"Hey," Phinn replied.

They quietly meandered through the rows of greenery so Phinn could teach Joshua how to care for each of the plants. Joshua took detailed notes the whole time, and asked all the right questions. Phinn knew the kid didn't have a green thumb or a hidden desire to garden, and that he was merely doing this for his sister.

"I feed the chickens first," Phinn explained. "It keeps them quiet while I water the plants and pick fruits and vegetables."

Phinn watched as Joshua pointed out the tomatoes and zucchinis and pame leaves that were ripe for picking. He was right each time.

"I talk to them sometimes," Phinn admitted. "Sometimes it's nice to talk about your problems without anyone interrupting with advice."

Joshua nodded in acknowledgment. He didn't say much throughout the rest of the lesson, but Phinn filled the silences. If he kept his mouth moving, it would prevent him from thinking about the vote. The ballots had to be in by noon, and it wouldn't take long to count them aloud.

"Do you have any other questions?" Phinn asked, after he watched Joshua hold his breath and carefully collect the eggs from the chicken coop. Joshua nodded, then said:

"Do you think she'll forgive me?"

"Who?" Phinn asked.

"Wylie. Do you think, if she's alive, she'll forgive me for taking your side before?"

Phinn wasn't sure how to respond. Wylie wasn't the most forgiving of people, but he could have been the perfect boyfriend, and he still wouldn't have been able to displace her brothers in her heart.

"You know Wylie. She usually blames herself, like with the accident in the Hamptons. In this case, I'm the only one to blame."

"Did you . . . have anything to do with the accident?" Joshua asked.

Phinn shook his head. He hadn't needed to destroy the Daltons' lives to convince them to come to the island. Even if their parents had been happily married and Joshua hadn't been a day away from going to juvie, they'd probably still have been lured by eternal youth and unlimited freedom.

"Did I tell you where we keep the baby three-legs?" Phinn asked, wanting to change the subject. "Wylie and Lola had quite the collection."

"Are you scared to grow old?" Joshua asked.

Of course he was scared. He'd been a teenager for more than three decades. He only knew how to take care of himself on the island. He hardly knew how to handle money.

Phinn couldn't imagine getting a job. He didn't have a high school diploma, and most of his life, he'd answered to no one.

"Yeah," Phinn admitted. "But I'll figure it out."

At least that's what Tinka had told him. The night before, she'd caught him sneaking into the Forbidden Side to pick *rahat* flowers and followed him in.

"Tinka." He'd said her name softly. "Come with me."

"No," she'd said. "If you're off the island, there's no reason to leave."

In the years they'd known each other, it'd been the first time Tinka had broken *his* heart.

"I'm in love with someone else," she'd gone on. "And I won't be there when the votes are counted. I don't care if it makes me arthritic. I don't want to say good-bye in front of everyone. So let's just do it now. I hate you, Phinn, but it is going to be weird to live without you."

"Right back at you."

They had hugged, but it was brief and awkward. It was hard to believe it would be the last time they'd ever see each other.

A shrill scream put an abrupt end to Phinn's memory. Startled, Joshua dropped the eggs from the coop, and they broke on the ground.

"*Someone's here!*" A voice shrieked.

Phinn recognized it as Bailey's. Joshua dashed out of the garden, and Phinn followed him. They arrived at the Clearing where they found Maz and a dozen or so residents already gathered. More were trickling in from the deck.

Bailey tried desperately to catch her breath, then frantically filled them in on what she'd seen.

"It's a boat. A big one. I was writing a song on the beach and I flew back here the second I saw it."

"How much time would you say we have?" Phinn asked.

"Ten minutes? Tops," Bailey replied.

"All the girls need to go into the panic room," Maz ordered.

"No!" Phinn said.

He'd recently bolted the floorboards in a symbolic gesture for Wylie. There was no way they could pull every nail out in time.

"I closed it off. But we need weapons. Bandit, take a team with you. Bring the entire supply."

Bandit didn't bother arguing with him or pointing out that they didn't take orders from him anymore.

"Do you think it's Hopper?" A terrified voice called out. Phinn wasn't sure who asked the question.

No, Phinn thought. Hopper and the rest of the lost kids were probably living a cozy life with a foster family somewhere on the mainland.

"Yes," Phinn said aloud. "It could be."

✦ ✦ ✦ ✦ ✦ ✦ ✦

WYLIE HAD BEEN RIGHT. IT WAS BETTER THAT NO ONE was hiding in the panic room. There was safety in numbers, and Phinn was glad the girls were standing behind him, gripping spears in their hands. Maz and Bandit wanted to plow through the trail and take their attackers by surprise, but Phinn insisted on playing defense.

"They could be passing by. Maybe they're lost. But if they see that the island's inhabited, they'll want to investigate," he argued.

If they flew toward people on a ship who were armed with guns, they'd take the residents out like a flock of game birds.

Phinn didn't dare say it aloud, but he hoped Wylie was on the boat and she had found someone to bring her home.

It was quiet long enough for everyone to let out a communal sigh, but just as they exhaled, the ground beneath them shook from approaching footsteps.

"Stand back," Phinn ordered. "Weapons at the ready." They all braced themselves, their spears poised.

See, Phinn wanted to say. *What would any of you do without me?*

No one had ever invaded the island. Sometimes, Phinn wondered if it was only visible to a privileged few. None of them knew how far its magical capabilities extended. Lola's tribe had claimed that adults couldn't survive on the island, but Phinn assumed that was a lie to help ease the pain of losing their parents. They'd intercepted several boats and sailors over the years, but managed to stave them off with clever lies and excuses for why they were there. The one that worked most often was claiming they were production assistants on an exclusive movie shoot. Any interlopers would shut down production, and face a hefty fine from the studio. Most people believed them and sailed away. Clearly, Hollywood was a very powerful force on the mainland.

Phinn was squeezing his spear so hard he thought he might accidentally snap it in half, when a handful of men wearing lab coats bombarded the Clearing. They were armed with handguns, drawn and ready to shoot.

Phinn suddenly regretted his decision not to import guns from the States. They were surprisingly easy to purchase, but random shootings were rampant on the mainland, and Phinn had always wanted life on the island to stay idyllic.

The men held up their weapons and pointed them at the residents.

"Hands in the air!" one of them said.

They didn't seem surprised to find dozens of teenagers staring back at them.

"Who are you?" Phinn asked. "What do you want from us?"

"*Hands in the air!*" The man yelled it this time.

Phinn nodded to the kids to follow orders. He put his hands up in surrender and dropped his spear in the process.

"No sudden movements," another person warned them.

A few of the men made their way through the crowd, checking to make sure no one had other weapons hidden on their person. Phinn stood still as they patted him down.

"Don't touch me!" Phinn heard Nadia shouting at one of the men. She flinched as he patted her down anyway, and another pressed a gun against her temple.

Put away the gun, Phinn wanted to yell. *That's not what's scaring her. It's your face.*

The creased skin, specks of salt and pepper stubble, and thinning hair were terrifying for the kids. After years of isolation, they were suddenly up close and personal with *adults*. For some, it would have felt less scary to be attacked by aliens.

Before Phinn could demand that the men tell him what they were doing here, a woman entered the clearing. She looked at least thirty years older than the kids, with faint smile lines and crow's feet, and gray roots peeking out beneath her tight curls. She was dressed in cargo pants and a long sleeved cotton T-shirt. She grinned at him.

"Hi, Phinn," she said as she looked him up and down. "Wow. You haven't aged a day since I last saw you. *Literally*."

Phinn tried to remember if they'd met on the mainland. Was she the mother of one of his recruits? Something seemed familiar about her face, but he couldn't place it.

"What's wrong?" the woman asked. "Don't you recognize me? I'm not as pretty as I used to be. You, on the other hand, are still as porcelain as ever. How lucky are you, toy soldier?"

Toy soldier. The nickname made Phinn's blood run cold. It was what she'd called him from the very first night they met. She was sixteen then. Phinn had crashed a party at her parents' mansion in east Hampton. He'd been amused as she drunkenly berated her grandmother in front of all the guests, and then stalked off to bed. Phinn had pretended he'd gotten lost among the endless maze of bedrooms and hallways, and stumbled into her outside her bedroom door.

"Where do you think you're going, toy soldier?" she'd asked him.

"I must be lost," he'd said.

They'd spent the rest of the night flying high on *parvaz* and bonding over adults who didn't understand them.

"What made you snap at your grandma?" Phinn had asked.

"She told me that women are meant to be nurses and not doctors. She refuses to pay for me to go to medical school someday. She's an old-fashioned hag."

It didn't take much to convince her to follow Phinn across the ocean. Not only would she get to stay young forever, Phinn had told her, but she could also practice medicine on the island. She'd even brought along a suitcase filled with cash from her parent's safe. It was enough money to keep the island fully stocked with items from the mainland for years.

Now the woman staring back at him barely resembled the teenager he'd once called his girlfriend.

"Olivia Weckler," Phinn said. "What are you doing here?"

"Oh, you know. I'm just here to take you and everyone else back to the mainland. What's that saying, Phinn? What goes around, comes around. It's a bit of a cliché, but I think it's fitting under the circumstances."

Phinn took a tentative step toward Olivia, but she backed away from him. He'd always feared this day. He always knew it would come. Someone would show up and try to destroy everything they'd built. It was already too late for him, but it didn't have to be too late for everyone else.

"Take me," he begged. "I'm the only one you're really here for. But leave the rest of the kids here. Please."

Olivia shook her head. "I can't do that, toy soldier."

Phinn had promised his friends that he'd protect them if anyone tried to invade the island. He grabbed Olivia by the collar, but someone behind him quickly pulled him away from her. He got a brief glimpse of a lab coat as a fist slammed into his gut. He tried to breathe through the pain, but the same fist punched him across the face and sent him to the ground. Phinn felt the back of his head hit the sand. Above, he could see the palm trees rustling in the breeze.

And then he saw her floating behind them. She was tiny, but he knew he wasn't seeing things. For a moment, he felt safe. After all, it was Tinka's face that always came into view when he *hadn't* died. Micah was perched in the air next to her.

Right before his eyes closed, he saw Tinka place a finger in front of her mouth.

"Shhhhhh," she warned him.

He tried to nod, but he couldn't lift his head. He felt a trickle of blood travel to his forehead and down his cheek. All he could do was let his eyelids shut. In that moment, he didn't even want Wylie there with him. The only person he wanted was his mom.

deserted
island

"I hate this stupid trail. Always have, always will," Zoe complained. "It's the longest hike *ever*."

Zoe reminded Wylie of her best friend Vanessa from back home. They both spoke in hyperbole no matter what they were discussing. Everything was always the "best" or the "worst" thing ever. At first, she'd found it charmingly familiar, but after nearly an hour of incessant whining, Wylie almost couldn't fault Phinn for locking Zoe up on the Forbidden Side. She was only tolerable in small doses.

"Someone please tell her to shut up," Sebastian groaned.

In close quarters on the boat, they'd bottled any tension and managed to avoid arguing. But right now, it felt like they might turn on each other and start their own war. They were all tired and hungry. They'd had another sleepless night on a ship, deciding to wait for daylight to explore the seemingly empty island. Wylie hadn't even bothered closing her eyes or deluding herself into thinking she could fall asleep. Rest would elude her until she found out if her brothers were okay.

As soon as the orange glow of the sun lit up the sky, the lost kids picked up their spears, stepped off the boat, and ventured toward the Clearing. This time, they wouldn't divide and conquer.

"Until we know what's going on, we stick together," Lola declared.

When Wylie and Hopper had returned to the beach and told the others that the island looked deserted, Lola's knees had buckled, and she'd gripped her belly as she vomited on the wet sand. Wylie held her hair back, and between retches, Lola had cried out Maz's name.

"It's okay. We're going to find him," Wylie had said, trying to soothe her best friend.

The Clearing looked even more trashed in the daylight than it had the night before. The waterfall had all but dried up. The tea lights had melted. Swamp-like algae muddied the lagoon's formerly glittery waters. Remnants of the memorial were scattered over the grounds. The lost kids were touched and amused by the messages they'd found from their old friends. Hopper chuckled when he saw his supposed HOPPER WAS HERE calling card carved into the trunk of one the trees. They were about to move on to the bungalows when Zoe let out a blood-curdling scream.

"There's a body in the lagoon!"

No, Wylie thought. *Please, God, no.*

Hopper followed the direction of Zoe's index finger and reluctantly approached the lagoon. Wylie and Lola followed close behind.

Through the grime on the surface, they could see someone floating on his or her stomach. Lola gagged and turned away to throw up again. Jersey and Hopper volunteered to remove the body, and the rest of them stood back as green murk spilled out from the edge of the lagoon. They flipped the corpse over as Wylie steeled herself for the worst.

None of them recognized the man staring back at them. His eyes were closed and his pruned skin had turned a shade close to periwinkle. "Who is he?" Wylie asked. Nobody had an answer.

The body was still wearing a lab coat with the word *BioLark* embroidered in orange thread and an image of a bird trapped inside a test tube on it.

"What do we do with him?" a terrified Charlotte asked.

"We leave him here for now," Lola said.

Next, they moved through the bungalows, and were relieved to find no signs of carnage or human remains. But most of the doors had been ripped off their hinges, and every drawer and closet had been ransacked. Several of the bungalows still had their doors secured and looked much tidier than the others.

"Someone's been living in these," Hopper pointed out.

There were suitcases full of clothing and toiletries, along with files labeled with the same emblem of a bird trapped inside a test tube, below the name *BioLark*. They sifted through the paperwork and discovered detailed notes about Minor Island, along with theories on how the island prevented inhabitants from growing old. The notes speculated that perhaps it was something in the water, the atmosphere, or the carbon dioxide released by the trees.

"It looks like someone went and blabbed about this place," Jersey said.

Wylie struggled to keep a nervous breakdown at bay. She had no idea who was behind BioLark and what their presence on the island meant for Joshua and Micah, but falling to pieces wouldn't do her brothers any good. She needed her sanity if she was going to find them.

Their next stop was the dining room. A layer of dust covered the tables and chairs, while remnants of cobwebs hung from the ceiling. It was Lola who noticed that none of the carefully carved spears were in their normal hiding place. Wylie ran straight to the floorboards that led to the panic room, but when she tried to pry them open, they wouldn't budge.

"Someone sealed the entrance. Phinn would never do that," Wylie said.

She pounded on the wood with her fists and screamed, "Is anyone in there? Can you hear me?"

But there was no response.

"What if they suffocated?" she said, frantically searching for a tool to tug out the nails. Hopper hurried to the kitchen and came back with a hammer. He fumbled as he tried to pull out the nails.

"This is a job better suited for someone with ten fingers," he confessed.

Charlotte took over, and to distract themselves from the agonizing wait, Lola and Wylie left to check on the garden. They tried not to dissolve into tears at the scene before them: every herb and plant and vegetable had wilted and died. But then they heard the sound of the chickens squawking and crying for them. They looked like they hadn't been fed in days, but they were alive.

"Hallelujah," Lola said.

They flapped their wings happily at Wylie, as she sprinkled mounds of wheat in the coop.

"Go to town," she told them. "We need to fatten you up again."

It was hard to say how long the island had been deserted, but someone had clearly been feeding the chickens until recently. They wouldn't have survived for more than a couple of weeks without sustenance.

Once they returned to the dining room, Charlotte only had a few more nails to remove. Hopper helped her lift up the door to the panic room, and Wylie didn't know whether to be relieved or distraught when they found it empty.

The *parvaz* field was silent when they came upon it, and while the leaves weren't completely shriveled up, they were on the brink of death. Wylie plucked a flower and was startled to notice another one didn't grow in its place. She reached for another *parvaz*, and gasped when she realized its vines were wrapped around a human hand.

It belonged to a middle-aged man, also wearing a BioLark lab coat. His tongue was hanging out of his mouth and he had a look of frozen terror on his face that seemed to disappear when they closed his eyes. The plants had wrapped themselves tightly around his neck—it looked as if the vines had smothered him. They needed to cover more territory and search the rest of the island for any signs of life.

Wylie felt wrong flying in the presence of so much death, but she didn't want to deprive the lost kids of their reunion with *parvaẕ*. Despite their drooping petals, the flowers still had the desired effect. The group soared away from the field. A bird's eye view gave them a broader scope of the overgrown jungles separated by trails of sand, but they didn't find any of their friends, even as they braved the Forbidden Side.

"We still have one more place to look," Wylie told the others as they landed in the Clearing. "Phinn's secret hut."

She met with blank stares. No one, not even Lola, knew about a secluded bungalow, and Wylie couldn't quite remember how to find the war room, hidden as it was behind layers of brush. They flew aimlessly for what felt like hours until, finally, Wylie spotted the rocky portion of the trail where she'd tripped and fallen with Tinka. It twisted and curved for about a mile before trees and thick ivy blocked the rest of the path. Wylie drifted to the ground and they followed her the rest of the way. A small opening already separated the ivy, but Hopper used his knife to widen the entrance, and helped each of them cross to the other side.

The log cabin was still intact. Perhaps no one in a lab coat had found their way to it. Lola's jaw dropped when she saw the place.

"I had no idea this was here," she confessed.

Wylie pressed the side of her body against the logs, but they wouldn't budge.

"Just give me a minute," she said.

Suddenly, the door burst open from the inside and someone tackled Wylie to the ground. Before she had time to react, the blade of a knife pressed against her neck. Tinka's crazed face was mere inches from her.

"No freaking way!" Tinka blurted. "Wylie Dalton?"

"In the flesh," Wylie managed to say.

Tinka put the knife away and stumbled off of Wylie.

"*Micah!*" Tinka yelled. "Get out here! It's your sister!"

Wylie had spent the last twenty-one days imagining this moment. It was the only thought that kept her going while she'd been biding her time in the middle of the ocean. Micah drifted out of the cabin. His face was covered in coarse stubble and he looked like he'd lost a few pounds. He didn't seem the least bit embarrassed by tears freely falling from his eyes. He and Wylie threw their arms around each other.

"You're alive," he sobbed into her shoulder.

"*You're* alive," Wylie answered.

"Either that or we're all dead and this is hell," Tinka broke in, her gaze landing on Hopper, Lola, and the rest of the lost kids. "What the hell is going on here? Where did you come from?" She brandished the knife.

"I've only got seven fingers left," Hopper said calmly. "I'd prefer to hold on to them if you don't mind."

Tinka dropped the weapon to the ground.

"He's not dangerous," Wylie assured Tinka. "He's . . . well, we have a lot of catching up to do."

"No shit," Tinka replied.

Before they could continue, another voice yelled out from inside the bungalow.

"*Help! Somebody! Get me out of here!*"

"Give it a rest, Dr. Jay!" Tinka yelled back.

"Who's that?" Wylie asked, not sure she wanted to hear the answer.

She peered inside the bungalow and saw a man, probably

in his late twenties, tied to a chair. He had distinctive eye-brows that offset his shaved but stubbled head. His brown eyes twinkled in the dim light, and his rich dark skin looked smooth and flawless. He wore a BioLark lab coat with a T-shirt of Albert Einstein underneath it.

"That's our hostage," Tinka said. "Say hello, Dr. Jay."

"Hello, Dr. Jay," he said, drily.

His eyes silently pleaded with Wylie before he spoke up again.

"I don't want any trouble," he said. "My colleagues are dead because of this awful place. I just want to go home."

It took four guys to lift up Dr. Jay in his chair and fly with him to the dining room. He begged for his life the entire way, and Lola assured him they had no plans to kill him. They sat him at the head of a table, his arms and legs tied together and tape covering his mouth. If it were up to the old Wylie, they would have untied him, but the Wylie of today knew not to trust as easily.

It was Lola who revealed to Tinka and Micah that Hopper was not the villain Phinn had made him out to be. He hadn't kidnapped anyone. In fact, he'd rescued each of the lost kids. The same way he'd rescued her and Wylie.

"Phinn left you to die?" Tinka asked Lola.

"Yes. I confronted him and he lost it." Lola shuddered at the memory. "Phinn doesn't want people around who are going to hold him accountable. I don't know why it took us so long to understand that."

Hopper shrugged. "You were brainwashed."

The events that had taken place since she'd left the island were a lot for Wylie to absorb: Phinn's impending exile, the return of Olivia Weckler, the trio of BioLark scientists who'd been left behind to collect evidence.

Micah and Tinka had hidden above in the palm trees as Olivia and her team injected the kids with syringes that put them to sleep, and then dragged them to a boat. Before most of the BioLark scientists departed for the mainland, they collected boxes of sugar roots and *parvaz* and *rahat* flowers, along with the herbs that were native to the island.

"I watched them take Joshua," Micah admitted, near tears again. "And I didn't do anything. I've never felt so arthritic in my life."

"You're not weak. There was nothing you could do," Wylie replied, though she couldn't be certain that was true.

"Olivia tried to find everyone," Tinka said, "but we hid in the war room, and she never found it."

Micah and Tinka had stayed hidden for days until they were desperate enough for food and water to brave the outside world. They came across the bodies in the *parvaz* field and the lagoon as they made their trek to the dining room, but it wasn't until after they'd eaten berries and vegetables that they flew to the Forbidden Side and found Dr. Jay.

"He was up to his waist in quicksand," Micah explained. "We rescued him, but then we had to take him hostage."

A rush of empathy took hold of Wylie as she recognized the look of fear and panic in Dr. Jay's eyes. Lola walked over to him and gently removed the tape from his mouth.

"*Please*," he begged. "Don't hurt me. I just want to get off this crazy island."

"What exactly were you assigned to do here?" Lola asked him.

Wylie lifted a cup of water to his mouth and allowed him to take a sip before he answered.

"Collect data, compile notes, and document any changes on the island. Olivia never told us it would be dangerous here. She called it paradise. She made it sound like we'd be taking a paid vacation. She even told us it might reverse the aging process."

"What happened to the other scientists?" Lola asked.

Dr. Jay bit his lower lip.

"I saw them die. Kevin and I were collecting *parvaz* samples when the vines wrapped themselves around his legs, and then his entire body. It happened so fast. We tried to save him, but they wouldn't let go. Then Charlie got sucked under the lagoon. I did everything I could to pull him out, but there was something in there that was much stronger than me. They were my friends and I couldn't save them."

Dr. Jay explained that, once alone, he'd gotten lost en route to the beach and found himself trapped in quicksand.

"It came out of nowhere," he said. "I would have died if your friends hadn't found me."

Lola nodded. "You were guinea pigs."

"What do you mean?"

"Olivia Weckler used to live here. She knew about the rumors that the island didn't take kindly to adults. That's part of the reason Phinn forced her to leave when we discovered she was aging. So she left you behind to see if the island really is dangerous."

Wylie had heard rumors about the island's discriminatory practices against adults. She never believed the stories she'd heard about the plants and trees and waterfalls that could defend themselves against interlopers who were older than eighteen. But now it seemed they had proof.

"No. . . ." Dr. Jay shook his head. "Olivia wouldn't do that to us."

"Think about it," Hopper added. "It would have been a lot easier to stay here than to drag fifty kids back to the mainland. Why not stick around and study them on the island unless she knew it was too dangerous?"

"We were expendable," Dr. Jay mumbled.

"If it makes you feel better," Charlotte piped up, "the rest of us can relate."

"Do you know where Olivia took our friends?" Wylie asked. "Do you know where she took my brother?"

Dr. Jay nodded. "I can help you find them."

"Why should we believe you?" Lola asked.

"Because," Dr. Jay said, "You don't have a choice."

* * * * * * *

IF WYLIE WAS RULED BY EMOTION, LOLA WAS RULED by logic. Wylie wanted to hike to the beach, get back on Hopper's boat, and be in New York by morning to storm the BioLark building and save Joshua. But Lola argued that they'd spent weeks planning Operation Exile, and needed at least a few days to come up with a proper plan to save their friends.

"*They're* the lost kids now," Zoe pointed out.

That night, everyone picked out bungalows they could comfortably sleep in. There were enough beds that had withstood the damage, and most of the kids were secretly thrilled to get to rest on mattresses and not on a boat that rocked back and forth. Dr. Jay seemed terrified by the prospect of spending one more night on an island that wreaked havoc on adults, so they assigned shifts to keep watch over him on Hopper's boat. Wylie and Lola found themselves back in their old room, and Hopper, not wanting to be alone, asked to sleep on their floor.

"Tell me about the Big Peach again," Lola said, sounding exhausted.

"It's the Big Apple, Lols," Wylie reminded her. Hopper let out a chuckle.

"That's what I said. The Big Apple. . . ."

Wylie sighed.

"That's not where we're headed. Dr. Jay said something about upstate."

"I'm not looking forward to going back," Hopper added. "If you're not careful, the mainland can eat you alive."

"Don't listen to him," Wylie said. "You'll be—"

Before she could finish making reassurances, Wylie heard Lola steadily breathing in and out. She was sound asleep. It had been a grueling day and they needed to give their minds a break.

Wylie was still worried about Joshua, but at least she'd been reunited with one brother. If someone had told her when she was marooned on a rock in the ocean that she'd wind up back in her room on Minor Island that Lola would be sleeping in the bed next to her, and that Hopper would be hanging out with them, she never would have believed it.

"Are you sad that Nadia wasn't here?" Wylie asked.

"Nah," Hopper said. "The fantasy is always better than the reality."

The floors of the bungalow made a creaking sound as Hopper rolled over to make himself more comfortable. A jar of fireflies added enough light to the room for Wylie to see Hopper twist his face in pain. After months of sleeping on the boat, he'd refused Wylie when she'd offered him the bed.

"Trade me places," she whispered now, careful not to wake Lola.

"No, I'm fine. Go to sleep."

"Foot to head, then," Wylie said. "Come on. It'll be better than sleeping on the floor."

"Not for you. My feet stink."

"I'll survive. Otherwise, you're gonna need a wheelchair when you wake up tomorrow."

But his feet didn't smell. They'd bathed in the ocean that evening, and were cleaner than they'd been in weeks. Wylie grazed her finger along the bottom of his foot, and he nearly kicked her in the face.

"Somebody's ticklish," Wylie said, giggling into her pillow.

"Goodnight, Dalton," Hopper replied.

"Goodnight, Hops."

Wylie turned her head away from Hopper's feet, and curled one arm under her pillow, but felt something sharp poke her elbow. She lifted up her pillow and discovered a note, neatly folded, and pulled it out, trying to be quiet.

It took her eyes a moment to decipher the words in the half-dark.

On the front, in pen, it read:

To: Wylie

From: Phinn

old friends

there were eight steps from the sidewalk to the front door of their brownstone. Gregory, in a hurry, usually took them two at a time, but today, getting to the top felt insurmountable. A wheelchair wasn't feasible. There were no ramps in their house, and Gregory's doctor had advised him that a cane would help speed up his rehabilitation. The apartment he'd rented after separating from Maura had an elevator, but he didn't want to sleep away from his children's home. It would feel like existing in an alternate universe. Like this is how his life would have turned out if he'd never met Maura, or if they'd stuck to their original decision to not have kids.

"Lean your weight on me," Maura said now. "We'll take it one step at a time."

Neither of them had broached the topic of their divorce since the kids went missing. It didn't make sense to argue over splitting up their assets when the three most important components of their lives together were gone. When their marriage had been at its worst, they'd still been able to look at Wylie, Joshua, and Micah, and be comforted by the fact that they'd raised three people who would do anything for each other. When Gregory watched his kids fall to pieces giggling together at some inside joke no one else found funny, he knew he'd at least done something right.

There were three more steps left before they reached the front door. Maura let out a heavy sigh, and mumbled under her breath:

"A sailing trip. You don't even like boats. What possessed you to leave when our kids are still missing?"

Gregory hadn't come up with a proper explanation for steering a boat into a storm, which had resulted in his near-drowning in the Atlantic. Part of him feared that if he told the truth, Maura would commit him to a psych ward and then he'd never be able to go back and rescue their kids.

"I needed time to think," was what he'd told her so far whenever the subject came up.

To Maura's credit, she'd only left his hospital bed to drop in at the Dalton volunteer center to check for any new leads on their children's disappearance that might get them through the day. A sketch of Phinn that identified him as a suspect in the kidnapping case was plastered throughout the streets of Manhattan, but no one had come forward with any information. There were days when Wylie's best friend Vanessa was the only person who showed up at the volunteer center to make more copies of flyers and answer the few phone calls that trickled in. Public interest about the three missing siblings from the Upper West Side seemed to have waned.

It was ten days after his accident that Gregory had the presence of mind to ask the nurse for his phone to call Olivia.

They'd been close friends when they both lived on the island. Several years after Olivia was exiled, Gregory left the island on his own accord and showed up at her front door. He asked if Olivia would take him in, and was quickly accepted as part of the Weckler family. Though they'd drifted apart over the years, she had money and resources, and was the only person who wouldn't think he was making up some elaborate story about magical islands and runaway kids. She'd agreed to meet him at the hospital the following day without giving any indication that she'd be willing to help him.

"You want me to go back to the island and bring your kids home?" she'd asked once he laid it all out for her.

Gregory nodded. "That's precisely what I'm asking."

She glanced at the photo of the map he'd stored on his phone.

"How do we even know this is real? Tinka could have made up these coordinates. If memory serves, she wasn't exactly the most trustworthy person."

Gregory thought back to the day, more than twenty-five years ago, when Tinka had slid the map in the front pocket of his jacket. She must have realized he was going to keep ignoring her apologies and pleas to stay. She told him she'd stolen the handmade map from Phinn's room. There was a stack of them, and she was sure Phinn wouldn't notice that one had gone missing.

"I think it's real," Gregory said. "It's at least worth looking into."

Olivia had said she needed time to think about it, but warned him not to get his hopes up. He was asking for a lot. But he was about to ask for more.

"I want you to bring them *all* back. Not just my kids," Gregory said. "Now I know what those other parents are going through. They've missed their children for a lot longer than I have. It's not right. They should be able to put their families back together."

Olivia's brow furrowed, and she sighed. "We were family once too, remember?"

"I remember," Gregory replied.

"You're asking for a lot. I'll need time to think about it."

"I understand."

The Wecklers had taken him in when he didn't have anyone, and Olivia had treated him like a sibling. He'd felt guilty when he'd quickly lost touch with her after he moved out, but he had needed to forget the island, and Olivia still hadn't back then. Even well into her twenties, she'd talked ad nauseam about the parties in the Clearing and the picnics on the beach, and even more about the people they'd both known, especially Phinn. Now that she was in her forties, he was glad to see she'd finally gotten over it.

Three days later, his phone rang.

"I'm going. I'll bring everyone back like you asked."

✦ ✦ ✦ ✦ ✦ ✦ ✦

THE FIRST FLOOR OF THE DALTONS' HOME HAD BEEN converted into Gregory's new sleeping quarters. With the help of some friends, Maura had moved the sofa and coffee table aside so they could comfortably fit a hospital bed in the living room. She'd also gone to the trouble of hiring a physical therapist to make daily visits and exercise Gregory's sprained hip until he didn't need a cane anymore.

"You can stay as long as you need," Maura said.

"Thank you," Gregory replied. He felt guilty for not telling her that he knew the identity of the suspect in the police sketch, but he wasn't sure if the truth about Phinn would bring her peace or anxiety. He doubted she'd believe him anyway.

"I think I'll take a nap, if you don't mind," he said now.

Maura helped him into bed and placed the crisp sheets over him. He knew how unfair this all was to her. He was the one who'd had an affair, and now here she was, being forced to take care of him. "In sickness and in health" didn't count when you were on the brink of divorce. He wanted to thank her, but the pain meds made him woozy and knocked him out with little warning.

The room was dark aside from a light in the kitchen when Maura gently shook him awake.

"You have a visitor," she said, her tone suspicious.

Olivia was standing behind her. It had been a week since she'd agreed to go to the island in his place. He could tell by the way Maura tried to gauge his reaction that she wondered if Gregory had invited his mistress into their home.

"Maura, this is Olivia," Gregory said, not sure how to

explain their connection. "She's a childhood friend."

"I'm also a doctor," Olivia jumped in. "I wanted to see if there was anything I could do to help. I know you've both been through so much. I'm so sorry about your children."

"Thank you," Maura said. "We have faith they'll be home soon."

Olivia nodded and smiled in response. It was the same look of pity and doubt that everyone seemed to give them.

"I'll be upstairs if you need me, Gregory," Maura added. Before Gregory's accident, she had spent hours each day sitting on their fire escape. No matter the weather outside, she seemed to think that the kids would sneak back in through Wylie's window one day. Once she was safely out of earshot, Gregory whispered to Olivia:

"Please tell me my kids are outside planning their entrance."

Olivia placed a gentle hand on Gregory's arm. She shook her head and looked down at her lap.

"We sailed for days, Gregory. We couldn't find anything. It's like the place doesn't even exist anymore. I'm beginning to think it was a figment of our imagination."

"It wasn't. You know that. You just didn't look hard enough," he said, trying not to raise his voice.

"I did my best," Olivia responded curtly. "If Phinn has them, there's no guarantee he whisked them off to Minor Island. I don't know what to tell you."

Gregory couldn't look at her, even though it wasn't fair to blame her for failing at something he hadn't been able to accomplish himself. He would get better in time. He'd get a new boat and avoid any inclement weather. He had the map. That should be enough.

Nothing would stop him until he found his kids and brought them home.

fear and loathing

wylie looked different. Not older exactly, but more grown up. Her long chestnut waves were swept up in a messy bun, her complexion had turned a darker shade of olive, and the summer dress she wore stopped right above her knees, revealing cuts and bruises sprinkled along her strong legs. Phinn expected her to look angry, but her demeanor seemed pleasant and welcoming instead.

"Wake up, sleepy head," Wylie said playfully. "You were snoring for hours, but I didn't want to disturb you."

Phinn was afraid if he spoke, the wrong words would tumble out of his mouth, and she'd remember the terrible things he'd done to her. So he kept his lips shut and placed his hand on Wylie's shoulder. Her body felt like ice beneath the heat of his palm.

"You're freezing," he managed to say. "Let me get you a blanket."

"I'm fine," Wylie replied.

He'd played their reunion over in his head a million times. What she would say, what he would say. He'd rehearsed his apology so often that he was afraid it might sound scripted and insincere when he said it aloud. But he wasn't prepared for Wylie's kindness right out of the gate.

"Why aren't you mad at me?"

Wylie laced her fingers through his hand and kneeled by his bed. She used her free hand to twirl his hair.

"Near death experiences have got a way of putting things in perspective. It made me realize that I can't live without you."

"I love you, Wylie," Phinn said.

"I love you," Wylie answered. She moved her lips toward him for a kiss, but suddenly her eyes narrowed. Phinn could see the smile evaporate from her face, as she pulled away from him in disgust.

"Wylie, what's wrong?" he asked.

She pointed her index finger at him.

"Your . . . your skin. You're getting *old*," Wylie said, horrified.

Phinn looked down at his body and watched as his skin rapidly shriveled up and became littered with liver spots. Patches of silver hair began to fall from his head, and inside his mouth, he could feel his teeth loosen and topple out. His vision blurred, but he could still make out Wylie slowly receding from him, as the steady rhythm of his heartbeat got slower and slower, and then faded all together.

+ + + + + + +

"*WYLIE!*" PHINN CRIED HER NAME, BUT SHE WAS NO longer next to him.

He blinked a few times, trying to adjust to the brightness of the bungalow. He was curled on his side, lying in his bed. Maybe he was still delirious from his dream, but his room looked smaller. Phinn was overcome by a sensation that the walls were closing in on him. The furniture looked the same, but something was off about it. It seemed somehow less worn, like it had been restored to its original state when it was new. He saw a twin bed against the opposite wall and realized he must be in someone else's bungalow. Phinn tried to sit up, but his ribs felt like they were stabbing his organs. He lay back against his pillow in search of relief, and noticed the palm frond roof had been replaced by white paint and plaster, a ceiling fan, and neon lights. He was so disoriented by his surroundings that it took him a moment to also notice the beeping of the heart monitor and the IV drip inserted in his forearm.

"Hello?" he called out. "Can anyone hear me?"

The door of his bungalow opened and a middle-aged man wearing scrubs and holding a clipboard walked in.

"Great, you're up," the man said. "We've been waiting to meet you."

"Who are you?" Phinn asked.

"I'm Nurse Conway," the man replied.

His skin was so pale that it was nearly translucent. Phinn could make out lavender veins in his eyelids and cheeks that made him look like he hadn't seen the sun in years. His hair, the color of tar, was long and knotted in a bun on top of his head.

"Don't worry," he went on, "We've been taking good care of you. Dr. Weckler said you deserved only the best."

The man took a syringe out of the front pocket of his scrubs, and tied an elastic band around Phinn's arm.

"What is that?" Phinn asked.

"Just morphine for the pain. You lacerated your spleen in an altercation with one of our staff members. You were bleeding internally. If it wasn't for Dr. Weckler, you'd be dead."

Phinn tried to move his arm away, but Nurse Conway was much stronger than his wiry frame suggested. He pressed Phinn's hand down on the bed, and pricked him with the needle. Within seconds, the sharp aching in his abdomen subsided.

"Get some rest. Dr. Weckler will be here shortly."

Nurse Conway left without telling Phinn where they were keeping him or how long he'd been confined to a bed. The last thing Phinn remembered was Olivia taunting him in the Clearing. Even with the morphine coursing through his veins, there was no way Phinn would fall back asleep. He wanted to get up and look out the window, but the curtains were drawn and he didn't have the strength to maneuver out of bed. The décor of the bungalow was strangely similar to his room on the island, aside from the extra bed and the narrow layout. Next to his bed, someone had taped a newspaper clipping, and he lifted his head to read it. It was about Wylie and her brothers going missing. Beside the article was a police sketch of his face.

"I thought Nurse Conway told you to rest, toy soldier," said a chipper Olivia as she entered.

"Don't call me that," Phinn replied.

Phinn still remembered the day he'd discovered Olivia was no longer one of them. They'd been napping on the beach and he'd woken up to find her still asleep beside him. As he ran his fingers through her copper-colored curls, he'd spotted several silver strands of hair gleaming in the sunlight.

Instantly, he felt like an idiot for letting his girlfriend take a sabbatical to the states so she could secretly pilfer more money from her family and travel cross-country. Trips to the mainland weren't a privilege he granted most residents, but he'd encouraged this one for selfish reasons. The Weckler family had unknowingly been funding him for years, and he'd gotten used to having cash ready when the island needed a new boat or supplies. Besides, he'd been ready for a break from their relationship, and granting Olivia travel privileges made it seem like the time away was her idea.

By the end of the year apart, he'd missed her carefree energy and was glad to bring her home to the land of sandy beaches and zero gravity. A few years later, lying on the beach together, he realized that she'd stayed on the mainland for far too long. And that because of it, she'd have to be exiled forever.

Olivia was the first to turn eighteen away from the island, and her misfortune saved the rest of them from making the same mistake. Phinn could still remember her high-pitched cries as Aldo and Maz dragged her onto the boat. Phinn had told himself she would eventually move on and forget about this place.

"How did you find us?" Phinn asked now.

Olivia, brimming with joy, explained that the police sketch had alerted Gregory to his children's whereabouts. He'd tried to sail to the island, but was critically injured after a storm tipped his boat over. If it hadn't been for the coast guard, Gregory would have drowned. And that's when he went to Olivia for help.

"Typical male," Olivia said. "He ignores me for years until he needs something. Well, I didn't feel obligated to help."

"But you still came to the island?"

"Things could have been much worse for you, toy soldier. Gregory would have had you thrown in jail, but I didn't tell him I found the island. He's not going to find us here. No one will."

"Where is *here*, exactly?"

"Would you like a tour?" Olivia asked.

"I suppose I don't have a choice," Phinn replied. He was equally curious and terrified to see what lay beyond the walls of the bungalow.

Nurse Conway entered with a wheelchair and carefully lifted Phinn into the seat. Thanks to the morphine, the aches remained at a minimum as he leaned back, Olivia pushing him.

As soon as they were out of the room, Phinn felt like he was trapped in a fun house. They were traveling down a rickety deck that looked like a distorted version of the one they'd built on the island. The path was shorter and narrower, and the wooden planks looked like they were made out of plastic. Each side was lined with bungalows that probably came with plastered ceilings and bad lighting just like the hut he'd been convalescing in.

"Where's everyone else?" Phinn asked.

"Don't worry. They're being well taken care of. You'll see them shortly."

Phinn looked up, half expecting to see clouds and sky, only to discover they were in an enclosed space. The ceiling was dome-shaped and lined with a projector screen. The lights and colors made it seem like the sun was setting, but it was just an optical illusion. Phinn glanced around, but couldn't find the projector that had created the façade of dusk.

"The sunset is just as beautiful here as it is on Minor Island," Olivia bragged.

"It's fake," Phinn pointed out.

"Not if you shift your perspective."

Phinn heard a *whooshing* sound as somebody flew past them toward the ceiling. He noticed the person wore scrubs and a lab coat.

"We did our fair share of foraging on the island before we brought you back here," Olivia explained. "My goal is to harvest *parvaz* and *rahat* flowers and put them into pill form. Just imagine being the first to offer people drugs that can take their pain away or make them fly."

Phinn knew *parvaz* had the potential to be a multi-billion dollar industry. He'd even considered selling the few he was going to take back with him to the mainland to earn enough money to rent an apartment.

"Are you hungry?" Olivia asked.

"Hungry" was an understatement. Phinn was famished.

He hadn't had a proper meal since dining on granola in the garden.

Entering the dining hall, Phinn felt like they'd emerged from a time machine that had transported them to the island circa 1988, the same year Olivia was shipped away. The room brought back memories of one of their most contentious arguments. On her trip back from the mainland, Olivia had broken the rules by smuggling in cassette tapes and a cassette player. He'd confronted her about the contraband in the dining hall, but she'd refused to give up the tapes and instead played him a song by a guy named George Michael. She'd begged him to slow dance with her, and somehow the combination of keyboard, drums, and vocals broke him down.

"How did you do all this?" Phinn asked now as he slurped chicken soup. "*Why* did you do all this?"

"Isn't it tropic?" Olivia replied. It seemed like she'd been waiting years for his approval.

"It's certainly impressive," was the most polite response Phinn could give, but a few other adjectives came to mind. Crazy and obsessive were good options. Olivia seemed pleased with his reaction, though.

"When my parents died, I inherited our family fortune," she explained. "By then, I was at a crossroads in my life."

"What kind of a crossroads?" Phinn acted like they were old friends catching up over lunch. The teenage Olivia had often gone from hot to cold without warning. If the adult version was the same way, then it was best to take advantage of her apparently cheery mood.

"It's a tad embarrassing," Olivia admitted. She blew on

her own bowl of soup and took a tentative slurp. "I was a doctor. I *am* a doctor, but I had my license revoked. My specialty was in pediatrics. I would see patients who were terminally ill and I kept thinking about the island. If only I could get them there; if they stopped aging, then maybe the cancer would stop progressing, too."

"Did you tell people about the island, Olivia?"

"I did," Olivia confessed. "But it sounded like a made up story. No one believed me. Everyone just assumed I'd gone insane. The more I told my patients' parents about a magical island populated by teenagers who don't grow up, the crazier they thought I was."

Olivia swirled her spoon inside the bowl of soup. Phinn got the impression she needed to contain her emotions before she could continue.

"There have been two times in my life when I lost everything. The first was when you forced me to leave the island. The second was when I lost the right to practice medicine. At least I didn't have to worry about money. I went on to build BioLark with the Weckler family trust. If living on the island wasn't an option, then maybe I could recreate it and figure out what kept everyone young. Maybe I could help people in the mainland and prove that I wasn't crazy in the process."

Or find a way to make yourself young again. Phinn did the math. She had to be pushing fifty by now, and she looked like she'd had work done to her face.

"How long have I been here?" he asked.

Phinn was always meticulous about keeping track of the number of days he spent on visits to the mainland. A million things could go wrong on a trip to New York that could keep him there past his eighteenth birthday, and he wasn't willing to take any chances. His plan was to stop making trips to the states once he had sixty days left to spare, just to give himself a wide buffer of time.

"A few days."

"When can I see everyone?"

"Soon. You and Maz are sharing a bungalow. He's been very worried about you. The others ask about you constantly."

Phinn shook his head. "I know you're lying. The rest of them hate me now. They wanted me to leave the island."

He wasn't entirely sure why he made the admission to Olivia. Maybe he thought it would gain him sympathy points or that they'd be able to commiserate about karma. Phinn could beg for forgiveness and say that he understood what he'd put her through so many years ago. But she didn't take the bait.

"Well, now we're all living in exile."

Olivia put down her spoon in her empty bowl. "What I want to know, though," she said to him, "is what happened to the rest of them."

"What do you mean?" Phinn asked, his face a mask of calm.

"There were some noticeable absences from the group we brought back. We scoured the entire island, but none of my men could find Lola, Tinka, or Wylie or Micah Dalton."

"I wish I could tell you," Phinn said. "We've had some issues with residents disappearing."

It wasn't a complete lie, but he couldn't tell if Olivia

bought it. He pushed his soup bowl aside and took a sip of water. He could smell cleaning fluid on the glass. Once they finished their lunch, Olivia revealed that she had a surprise waiting for him and carted him out of the dining hall.

"Close your eyes," she said, as they were about to round a corner on the deck.

Phinn did as he was told.

"Are they closed?" she asked with the excitement of a kid skipping through the gates of an amusement park.

"Yes, Olivia."

The wheelchair jutted forward, rocking back and forth over uneven plastic, then slowed to a stop. Suddenly, Phinn heard music. It was Bailey's voice singing what had become an anthem of sorts back home.

> *Old enough to fight a war, but still too young*
> *   to drink*
> *Why abide by rules and laws that tell us how*
> *   to think?*
> *Seventeen forever and living on our own.*
> *Blame it on our parents,*
> *They reaped what they have sown. . . .*

"Okay," Olivia said, "you can open them."

Phinn would have preferred to keep them shut. The off kilter replica of the Clearing was smaller in scale and the positioning of the lagoon and waterfall weren't right. The lagoon was such a bold shade of blue that it looked like buckets of dye had been poured into it, but the unappealing hue wasn't stopping Helen and Nadia from swimming in it. Phinn spotted Joshua and Maz helping themselves to what looked like sugar root mocktails. Olivia had probably pilfered the ingredients from the island.

"Splash!" They shouted as they clinked their cups. They seemed inexplicably happy.

If Phinn squinted his eyes, he could almost make believe they were home. Except that in this version of the Clearing, the kids wore hospital scrubs and adults in lab coats milled about, watching their every move.

"Surprise!" Olivia said. "It's your very own residency party. Welcome to your new home."

Olivia cupped her mouth with her hands and yelled out to the group:

"Phinn's back!"

She carried herself with the same exuberance she had as a teenager. It had been charming and contagious back then, but witnessing the same energy from an adult in this weird fake place was sadly comical.

The kids stopped what they were doing and looked at Phinn in unison. Their movements were so in step with each other that it felt like the entire moment was rehearsed or choreographed. The greeting only got more bizarre when they cheered for him. They were supposed to hate him. They were supposed to vote him off the island. Maz leaped into the air and landed on the stairs where Phinn was sitting.

"We missed you, brother!" he said, tossing his arms around Phinn and giving him a hug.

"I don't understand," Phinn replied. "They hate me."

"Pish-posh," Olivia dismissed. "You're their fearless leader, Phinny."

No one had ever called him Phinny but his mom. He almost asked Olivia to stick to "toy soldier," but a part of him loved hearing his childhood nickname again.

"Maz, tell him how happy you are here," Olivia encouraged.

Maz's face lit up with a smile. His eyes sparkled in a way they hadn't since Lola's disappearance.

"What's not to love? BioLark's been great to us."

Maz took a *parvaz* out of his pocket and tossed it at Olivia. She playfully caught it in her mouth. Phinn couldn't shake the notion that he was trapped in an alternate universe. Between their perky dispositions and the glossy surroundings, it felt like his friends were turned into mindless robots.

"We've been waiting for you to join the party," Maz added.

He handed Phinn a *parvaz*, and Phinn promptly swallowed it. He needed a break from beds and wheelchairs. Within minutes, he fluttered up in the air. He flipped onto his back and looked up at the ceiling. It had gone from cotton candy pink to a burned charcoal. Tiny stars began to glow from every corner. Phinn waded through the air with his arms until he got higher and higher. He reached with his fingertips and touched the screen. It felt like being held hostage inside a planetarium.

Maz followed closely behind him. A few feet away, an oblivious Olivia did back flips and yelped with joy. Phinn noticed a necklace slip out from the safety of her sweater and dangle from her body. As he inched closer, he realized it was the one that had belonged to his mother. The same piece of jewelry he'd given to Wylie the morning after prom night. Olivia must have stolen it from his pocket after bringing them here. His first instinct was to fly toward her and reclaim his property, but Maz pulled him back before he could. He placed his lips next to Phinn's ears and whispered so low that Phinn wasn't sure he heard the words correctly.

"We're going to die here unless you get us home."

confessions of a dangerous mind

within a day of their return, the *parvaz* field slowly hummed and crackled again. The garden was already thriving. The vegetables and sugar roots had renewed their lease on life. The pame leaves were the palest shade of lavender, but they were growing darker by the hour. New eggplants were bulbous and ripe for picking. Wylie sliced them open and soaked them in water and sea salt to remove any residual bitterness. She'd been awake since dawn, collecting and prepping the ingredients for Sweet Honey Stew. The clock was ticking to complete the recipe by sundown for their journey to the mainland, but Wylie didn't mind spending most of the day in the kitchen. She'd forgotten that preparing a meal was her preferred method of meditation. The repetitive motion of the knife distracted her from thinking about Phinn's note. Wylie kept the letter in her back pocket, but hadn't found the nerve to read it. And she hadn't mentioned its existence to anyone else. Instead, she focused on supplying her friends with the meals they'd fantasized about in exile. Lola was the most eager for Sweet Honey Stew, since Phinn was no longer able to stop her from eating her childhood favorite. But she'd been complaining of nausea, so Wylie added a generous helping of sliced mint leaves to help settle her stomach.

"I won't be able to hold it down," Lola said, as she watched Wylie toss the vegetables into a pot of boiling broth.

"It'll make you feel better. My dad used to cook it for me any time I felt sick," Wylie said.

"I'm not that kind of sick. It's anxiety. The only thing that will cure it is seeing Maz again."

Wylie smiled and nodded. She didn't dare say so out loud, but she was jealous of Lola. She envied the fact that her friend was one half of a stable relationship, even apart. It must be nice to believe in things like love and forever. It must be nice to trust someone to the point that you felt ill without them.

Lola took a few sips of the soup, but refused the rest when it seemed like her insides wouldn't tolerate it.

"Don't waste your cooking on me," she said. "Save it for the kids who are staying behind. Charlotte's the only one who knows how to put a meal together, and her food is still barely passable."

The lost kids hadn't shown much desire to leave the island to rescue those who'd held them prisoner. As far as they were concerned, they had what they wanted: their island back. So Lola decided it was best they stay behind to repair the bungalows, take care of the chickens, and nurse the herbs and vegetables. That left Wylie, Hopper, Lola, Tinka, and Micah to carry out the rescue mission.

Dr. Jay was their only way into BioLark. They'd been making sure he was well fed, properly hydrated, and had a warm place to sleep in the cabin of Hopper's boat. Wylie hoped he was a fan of eggplant.

Once the vegetables had cooked and softened, Hopper volunteered to carry the heavy pot of stew to the boat, while Lola and Wylie trailed behind him. It was strange to see him roaming around on dry land. The ship was claustrophobic, and yet he still preferred to pass the time there. On his rare visits to the island, he took up far more space.

"What?" he asked when he'd catch Wylie staring at him.

"Nothing," she'd always reply.

But she wanted to tell him that he seemed like a different person. Happier, lighter, carefree. The last time he was here, he'd been crammed in a jail cell. Of course he'd want to swing his arms, widen his stance, and leap up the stairs two at a time. She liked this side of him. She didn't want it to go away.

"We come bearing gifts," Hopper crowed as they made their way into the cabin of the boat.

Dr. Jay sat on the bed, poring over the BioLark binders while Tinka and Micah stood guard. For the last three afternoons, they'd gathered here for briefings on Olivia Weckler. Dr. Jay said he believed in transparency, but he also believed in saving his own ass. Which was precisely why he wouldn't reveal everything he knew about their destination.

"I'm not about to make myself expendable," he explained

during their first briefing. "I'm sure y'all are good kids, but that doesn't mean you won't leave me here to die."

Even though he'd told them that the lab was located in upstate New York, he wouldn't say *where*. The only way they'd be able to get to BioLark was with Dr. Jay acting as their GPS.

Wylie wouldn't admit it to Lola or Hopper, but she liked having an adult in their midst. Something about being in the presence of Dr. Jay made her feel safe. She could tell that Hopper liked him, too. They'd both grown up in the foster care system and though Dr. Jay had more than a decade on Hopper, they had some of the same caseworkers in common.

"I can't believe you knew Sherry Hinton!" Hopper had exclaimed. "She was always my favorite. The woman couldn't sugar coat things if she tried."

"Sherry's a rare gem. She's what you guys would call 'tropic.' She drove three hundred miles just to come to my med school graduation."

According to Dr. Jay, Olivia had a tendency to hire employees who had no families.

"We don't even have to commute to work because we live there. It seems crazy when I say it now, but it didn't feel crazy when I got the job. It felt like work was my family."

Dr. Jay had a dimple in each cheek that appeared at the smallest hint of a smile. His lashes seemed to go on for miles, and he had a nervous twitch that involved biting his lip and placing a finger to his chin. If Wylie were still capable of trusting her gut, she would have been confident that they were in good hands. But months ago, she'd thought the same of Phinn. Now every intonation and every gesture made her wonder whether Dr. Jay was someone who would help them or destroy them. Those lines seemed increasingly blurred.

Wylie poured him a bowl of stew and he complimented the aroma of mint as he took his first bite. His dimples came into full view.

"It's good," he said. "Thank you."

"You're welcome," she replied. It was nice to be reminded that she was good at something.

"Have you come up with any more options for us?" Hopper asked.

"Nope. I keep coming back to the same conclusion: you're either looking at a quick fix or a long con," he told them.

The quick fix meant going to the authorities as soon as they docked their boat in New York. There were several problems with this plan. First, it required telling the world about the island. Once their parents and family members learned of their true whereabouts, it would be close to impossible to sail back to the island and stay seventeen forever. Wylie's mom and dad would never let her or her brothers out of their sight if she turned herself into the police. It was hard to imagine leaving Minor Island without any assurance that she'd find her way here again.

"That's not an option."

It was Micah who said what they were all thinking.

"We've gotta find a way to bring everyone home without exposing ourselves in the process. We have lives here,"

Micah added with a glance toward Tinka. "We can't let some bitter old lady take that away from us."

"Then," Dr. Jay replied, "we enter the lion's den. I bring you to BioLark on a silver platter. At least that's what it'll have to look like. Olivia's all ego. She's the smartest person I've ever met, but she's also deeply insecure and she needs validation. You wait until she gets comfortable. You wait until she feels like you *love* her. Like you owe her a debt of gratitude. You wait until she's least expecting it, and then you pounce."

He'd already warned them that the facility was filled with security cameras and audio bugs. Surveillance was Hopper's area of expertise on the mainland, and based on Dr. Jay's descriptions of the spy ware, he'd been able to confirm that BioLark would monitor every word that came out of their mouth. No conversation was safe. They were always watching and listening. An uprising would have to take place when the staff was least prepared for it and a swift exit was critical.

"There's only one entrance into the facility that I know of, but Olivia's always claimed there were underground tunnels," he added.

"Tunnels?" Tinka asked. "You've been keeping that one in your pocket."

"I told you," Dr. Jay said, "I'm not giving all the goods out at once. There are a few other nuggets that I won't parcel out till you get me the hell out of here."

He explained that Olivia wanted them to have safe passage out of the building if they ever needed to make an emergency exit. It seemed not everything that happened at

BioLark was legal, and Olivia was always afraid of being found out by the government. But she was also the only person who knew how to access the tunnels. Dr. Jay had no idea where they started or where they ended up.

"It might just be some elaborate maze below ground with dead ends at every corner. But if you can play along, then I'll have time to find out. Once I have an exit strategy, I'll get everyone out. Olivia has morning staff meetings, which will only leave us with a few guards to outmaneuver, and then we'll make our escape."

"You're asking us to put a lot of faith in you," Wylie couldn't help pointing out. "Why can't you just take us into the lab and we'll force Olivia to let our friends out?"

Dr. Jay laughed. "You think it's gonna be that easy? How old are you?"

"Seventeen," Wylie answered. She hated being condescended to by people who were older than her.

"Well, Olivia's waited *thirty* years to get to Phinn and find the island. She's not going down without a fight. If you go in swinging, she'll swing harder. She'll blow the place up before she lets your friends out."

If everything Dr. Jay was saying was true, then they had to listen to him. They agreed they'd enter as hostages and wait for Dr. Jay to make the next move. Before they ended the briefing, Dr. Jay grabbed a pen and asked for intel on Minor Island to scribble on his forearm.

"Why?" Hopper asked.

"I have a tendency to lose notepads. I jot down notes on my arm, because then I won't misplace them. Olivia knows this about me. If she doesn't see any pen marks on my arm, then she'll figure something's up. Sometimes I write them in code. Once we're on the other side, they might be the only way I'll be able to communicate with you."

They spent the next few minutes shouting out benign facts about the island, and Dr. Jay wrote them down until his arm was covered in ink.

"We're good," he declared. "Olivia won't suspect a thing."

✦ ✦ ✦ ✦ ✦ ✦ ✦

THE AFTERNOON SUN BEAT DOWN ON THEM AS THEY left the cabin. Micah and Tinka volunteered to load the boat with blankets and pillows and other supplies that would help ease an evening at sea.

"Bring a barf bucket too," Lola requested. She gave Wylie a hug, and then flew off to their bungalow for some much-needed rest before their departure.

Hopper and Wylie had already completed their to-do list for the trip, and filled the remaining hours with a picnic on the beach to watch the sunset. Hopper brought his guitar and belted out one of their favorite Youth Brigade songs. If he'd been a contestant on one of those singing competition shows, the judges would have praised his flawless pitch.

"For years I tried to convince myself that this place actually sucked," Hopper said. "I guess it made it easier to imagine never living here again."

"I wish it did suck," Wylie said. "Then it wouldn't be so hard to leave."

The sharp corner of Phinn's note poked Wylie in the

thigh. She'd stored the letter in her pocket; partially hoping it would fall out during a flight and disappear forever so that she'd never have to read it. What difference would it make if she knew whatever Phinn wanted to say to her? She wanted nothing to do with him. She didn't *care* about his feelings.

"Earth to Dalton," Hopper said, squeezing her shoulder. "Where did you disappear to?"

"Sorry," Wylie replied. She grabbed the note from her pocket and handed it to him.

"This was under my pillow in the bungalow. I haven't read it yet. I keep wanting to throw it away. But maybe there's something in here that could help us."

Hopper turned the note over in his hand. They hadn't spoken much about Phinn since arriving on the island. She watched as he contemplated the folded piece of paper and hoped he wasn't hurt that she'd kept it to herself.

"Forget it," Wylie said. "Let's throw it in the ocean."

Hopper shook his head. "No. I think you should read it."

He offered the note to Wylie, but she couldn't take it. Finally, they agreed that Hopper would read it aloud.

Dear Wylie,

By the time you get this, I'll no longer be living on the island. You'll probably be thrilled to hear that. My mistakes caught up with me and no one wants me to stay. I can't say I hold that against them. This is my home, and there will be so much I'll miss about living here. Mostly, I'll miss the people. I'd be lying if I said I wasn't scared of growing old. The most magical thing about Minor Island isn't just the fact that we get to be teenagers forever, but it's that we never lose our youthful idealism. I'm not looking forward to giving that up as the years go by. But all that pales in comparison to the hardest part of leaving the island: wondering if I'll ever get to see you again.

I've had a lot of loss in my life. I'm not trying to make excuses for my choices and decisions. Your dad hurt me when he sailed away from the island, but it was only because I hurt him first. We were as close as brothers when he left. I was angry and upset, and I didn't get over it until I met you.

I was struck by you at that party. I didn't need to fake that. And the more I got to know you that night, the more I liked you. I never intended for that to happen, but I couldn't help it. You're loyal, caring, smart, funny, stubborn in all the best ways, and ridiculously strong. I'm not sure you realize that last part. Being around you made me realize why grown-ups on the mainland want to get married and start families. I would go to sleep at night thinking about us having a life together away from the island. As much as I loved seventeen-year-old Wylie, and as much as I thought you loved seventeen-year-old Phinn, I was curious to know what twenty-something Phinn and Wylie might be like. What would we be like in our thirties and forties? In our eighties and nineties? I liked to imagine how we would change and how we would stay the same.

But I loved you too much. I became terrified that you would be taken away from me. You would be another loss. I thought the only way I could prevent that from happening was if I controlled everything. I thought we could get to a place where, once I did tell you the truth about your dad, it wouldn't matter so much. None of it came out the way I intended.

Then I thought I could bully you into forgiving me. I was an idiot, obviously.

I don't know a thing about love. I don't know how to be selfless. I don't know how to love unconditionally. I don't know how to be honest when the truth scares the hell out of me. I don't know when to let go. I don't know how to let people down gently. I don't know how to show the worst parts of myself, and still think someone could love me. No one stuck around long enough to teach me any of that. You came the closest. And yet, as I write this, I wish I could go back to that night in Brooklyn and do everything differently. If I could do it all over again, I wouldn't disrupt your life. Unlike the rest of us, you have parents that love you. It was wrong of me to take you away from them. It was wrong of me to rob you of experiences you'll never get to have on the island. Your future is brighter than this place. I bet it includes Michelin stars and rave culinary reviews and prouder than proud parents.

It might sound crazy, but I know you're safe. I can't help thinking that if you were dead, I would somehow feel it. The world has meaning and I

think that's because you're still in it.
I'm not convinced we'll ever see each
other again. I don't think I'll ever get
a response to this letter, and you may
never read it. I also don't expect it to
change anything. But no matter how
long I live on the mainland, you'll
always be the love of my life. And I
hope to God I'm not yours. You
deserve so much better.

Love,
Phinn

Wylie wanted to rip the paper to shreds, set it on fire, and spit on the ashes.

"You don't have to hate him because of me," Hopper said. "You're allowed to have your own opinion."

"I don't hate him for you, Hopper."

She hated that Phinn's parting resurrected feelings she'd buried so deep and so long ago, she'd forgotten they'd even existed. Why did Phinn get to have the last word? Why did he get to play on her empathy? He had no right to explain himself. And he had no right to make her feel guilty for leaving her parents or make her question whether she belonged on Minor Island. It was a convenient argument from someone living in exile. Even in his good-bye letter, he was trying to manipulate her into being with him.

"It's not fair," Hopper mumbled.

"What's not fair?"

Hopper collapsed on the beach and let out a sigh.

"That Phinn got to be with you before . . ."

But he didn't finish the thought and he didn't have to. Wylie knew what he wanted to say. It wasn't fair that Phinn got to be with her when her heart was open to love and all its possibilities. It wasn't fair that he got to know the Wylie who could show affection freely. It wasn't fair, because Phinn was the person who destroyed that girl. Everyone else would be left with a person who took everything they said with a grain of salt, and was too traumatized to love with abandon.

"You're right," Wylie agreed. "It's not fair."

She lay down in the sand next to him and her fingertips touched the stumps on his right hand. Sometimes it was so easy to be his friend and sometimes it felt nearly impossible.

"Phinn was right about one thing," Hopper said. "He won't be the love of your life."

Wylie nodded. It felt like the perfect time to roll over on her side and kiss him, but she cared about him too much to do that. Hopper had been deprived of so much in life. He deserved a girl who *was* open to love and all its possibilities. A girl who *could* show affection freely. He deserved more than Wylie.

The stars were beginning to brighten up the graphite-colored sky. They didn't talk about Phinn again as they flew to the Clearing and said their good-byes to the lost kids. No one could bring themselves to get too sentimental. The more casual the farewell, the more it felt like they'd see each other again.

As Hopper steered the boat away from the dock, Wylie and Micah stood at the stern and kept their gaze fixed on the beach. Though the time of day was different, the line where the ocean met the sand looked as radiant as the day Phinn had brought them here. Wylie tried to memorize every inch of the image. From her current vantage point, no one would ever be able to tell that hearts had been broken among the lush greenery. Or that lagoons and *parvaz* flowers could kill you in your old age. No one would know that kids had been locked up in cages on the Forbidden Side and tortured till their spirits were broken. No one would know that the Wylie who entered the island a few months ago was an entirely different person from the Wylie who was leaving it now.

"Three hundred and forty-two days," she said aloud.

"Until what?" Micah asked.

"Until I'm technically eighteen," Wylie replied.

"We'll be back before then," her brother reassured her. "Me, you, and Joshua."

And no Phinn.

Wylie smiled at the thought. But once the beach and palm trees disappeared from view, her mind shifted to Phinn's letter and the ways she wanted to respond to him. She couldn't quiet the imaginary argument between them in her head.

You're wrong, she told Phinn. I belong on the island. I don't need Michelin stars or rave reviews. And I don't need proud parents.

The Phinn in her fantasy gave her a knowing smirk and said:

Keep telling yourself that, Wylie Dalton.

fine wine

back home, Phinn used to wait until everyone was asleep before tiptoeing out of his bungalow and walking down the rickety steps to the Clearing. It was late enough by then that even the insomniacs had retired to their huts. The fireflies weren't bright enough to light his path, so he became accustomed to using a torch. The wooden branch was heavy, but at least it could double as a weapon if need be. Plus, it was good exercise to sprint down the trail to the Forbidden Side. With the help of *parvaz*, he'd float over the fence and gracefully land on the other side. The flames of the torch made it easy to avoid the quicksand and find the patch of *rahat* flowers that sprung up around the cages. He hated those flowers. If he could figure out a way to poison their roots so that they'd never grow again, he would have. He considered setting them on fire, but was afraid the entire island would go up in smoke. So instead he resorted to plucking them one by one and hiding them under his bed until they died. He wouldn't let them take anyone away from him again.

But now they were taking *everyone* away. Some days, he even had trouble recognizing himself. They'd all gone from teenagers to lab specimens who were prodded and pricked and plied with drugs. They drifted around the poorly constructed Clearing like a pack of melancholy zombies who didn't even have the initiative to eat brains. The *rahat* flowers made him feel like an empty vessel, and the high dose of *parvaz* had him longing for solid ground. He never thought he could get sick of flying, but the BioLark staff had taken something magical and turned it into a cruel endurance test. Floating through the air for hours felt like a marathon without the medals or adoring crowd at the finish line. No one would explain the reasons for the experiments, but Phinn and Maz had their theories. After hours of testing, they stayed awake as long as they could in their bungalow. By the middle of the night, the drugs seemed to wear off and they could think clearly again.

"They're trying to figure out the exact dosage for *parvaz*," Maz speculated. "If they're going to make it into a pill, they'll need to know how much you have to take to make it last all day. And the *rahat* flowers are an added bonus to weaken our resolve."

"No," Phinn disagreed. "Olivia wants to make a painkiller. They're all the rage on the mainland. If she calls her version 'homeopathic,' then she'll have a leg up on the competition."

"Why can't she find other people to experiment on?" Maz asked. "Why us?"

"Isn't it obvious?" Phinn said. "Revenge."

That night, as they fought off much-needed rest, their theories turned to Wylie and Lola. Neither of them was willing to assume the worst. It was nice to at least get to tell someone how he planned to apologize to Wylie if he ever saw her again.

"She'll forgive you," Maz said, though they both knew that the chances of that happening were slim. "Maybe she found Hopper's boat and rescued Lola from his clutches. Maybe they're back on the island by now, wondering what happened to us."

Phinn was glad it was dark inside their room so Maz couldn't see the shame and guilt written on his face. He allowed his breathing to grow heavy, and hoped that Maz didn't wonder why he always fell asleep when the subject of Lola came up.

The following morning started the same as every other one. They were woken up by Nurse Conway and sent to the dining room for tiny cartons of store-bought orange juice and milk, accompanied by a bowl of bland and lumpy oatmeal. Olivia greeted them with a cheery smile and the generic mantra of the day.

"Today is the first day of the rest of your life," she announced.

The kids lifted up their beverages and shouted "hear, hear!" in unison.

At first, Phinn worried his friends had contracted a fatal strain of Stockholm syndrome that fooled them into thinking they liked being here. But then, on his second morning, he'd made a show of dumping out his orange juice after

Olivia declared that "when life gives you lemons, make some lemonade." It was a minor act of defiance, but the bodies around him went rigid. His friends were afraid for him. It was Nurse Conway who put a hand around his neck and choked him, while Olivia lectured him about treating his elders with respect.

"There are starving children all over the world, Phinn," she said. "You should be grateful to have a roof over your head and food in your belly."

Phinn wasn't sure the meals they were eating could actually be classified as food. It seemed that flavor should be a requirement when it came to anything edible. Nurse Conway let go of his neck and Phinn gasped for air. Once he could finally speak, he knew to apologize profusely.

The experiments started promptly after breakfast. They were escorted to the clinic and forced to stand in two lines. The nurses gave the boys three doses of *parvaz* and *rahat*. The girls received half the amount. Olivia liked to call it her version of the birth control ritual.

None of them tried to hide the flowers under their tongues or pretend to swallow. There was no point. The nurses and orderlies were thorough and always checked their mouths to make sure they ingested the dose. And anyway, they were grateful for the drugs. They needed them to withstand the experiments, or "daily activities," as Olivia preferred to call them. The benign name made what they were doing seem far less unethical. Their "activities" always included hours of flying in circles below the saturated sapphire dome decorated with animated clouds. The staff followed them and checked their vitals every thirty minutes. Combining the flights with *rahat* flowers made their muscles cramp less from the constant movement.

The afternoon activities always varied. Sometimes they were forced to lie in bed while a nurse collected tissue and hair samples. Sometimes they had to submit to urine testing. There were CAT scans, iodine patch tests, and fertility exams. Phinn had heard from Nadia that the girls were given hormone shots so that BioLark could retrieve and freeze their eggs. He didn't know how they smiled their way through it all, and wished there was something he could do to make it stop. Phinn hated the unpredictability of the afternoons. The evening's individual evaluations were even more extreme, but at least he knew what to expect.

"Can you feel that?" Olivia asked. She was always the one who conducted his session.

Phinn shook his head. "I don't feel anything," he said.

As soon as the ceiling in BioLark turned to dusk, each of them was taken to a private room and connected to a heart monitor for what Olivia dubbed *punire* tests, which Phinn knew was the Latin verb for "to punish." The tests included a prick of a needle, an electric shock, a knife dragged across the small of their back, or a lit cigarette pressed into their skin. It supported Phinn's theory that BioLark was developing its own form of painkillers, and that they needed to see how well *rahat* suppressed the damage they were inflicting. Or maybe Olivia and her cohorts were just a bunch of sadists. Either way, the drug made their nerves numb enough to withstand the tests, but did nothing to help with the cuts, burns, and bruises that were marring their formerly youthful flesh. The scars Phinn had before the experiments were no longer visible beneath his new wounds. But Phinn would have gladly accepted a thousand more cuts if it meant he could skip the interrogation portion of the sessions. Perhaps Olivia was trying to figure out if *rahat* also eased emotional pain.

"Where's Wylie Dalton? What did you do to her?"

Olivia always asked the same questions, and Phinn always declined to answer. Tonight was no different.

"How old were you when your parents died?" she continued.

"Five. I was five when my parents died."

"And how did they die?"

Back when Olivia lived on the island, she was always badgering him about his mom and dad. She complained that Phinn had too many walls. She seemed to think that if she could get to the root of how he lost his parents, she could be the first girl to heal him of the trauma.

"They killed themselves," Phinn muttered, as his heart monitor remained steady.

"How?" she asked. This time, the monitor made high-pitched beeping sounds and Olivia marked down notes on her clipboard.

"No comment."

By nighttime, they were subjected to the most demented activity: a party hosted by Olivia. All they wanted to do was retire to their bungalows and go to sleep, but Olivia insisted on the late night soirees. Didn't she have a life outside of her work? A partner or children? Didn't she have anywhere else she'd rather be?

It had been ten days since she'd plucked them from

the island and, apart from when they were sleeping, the BioLark staff lingered nearby at all times. Even when they were alone, Phinn assumed their conversations were being listened to. Phinn wished he'd done more on the island to prepare them for a kidnapping of this scale. If only they'd developed a secret language they could use to covertly plan an uprising. Phinn and Maz called the revolt they wanted to organize "prom night" and kept their conversations as vague as possible.

"We'll have to wing it," Maz whispered the night before.

Phinn had nearly laughed. Rebellions may have been improvised along the way, but they needed some level of planning and organization. Neither he nor Maz had spotted an exit out of the building. Even if they could get outside, there was no way of knowing how to get away or where they were. Sedated on Minor Island, they'd all woken up with no idea how they'd arrived here. It was right out of Phinn's own playbook.

But Maz was right. They didn't have the luxury of planning their rebellion. Their only option was to lead by example and hope everyone else followed suit. The kids outnumbered the BioLark staff two to one. There were strong girls and boys among them. The teenagers could take over the place and force their way out.

* * * * * * *

"THANK YOU FOR ANOTHER GREAT DAY ON BIOLARK'S Minor Island!" Olivia shouted to everyone from the top of the waterfall. "I speak for our entire staff when I say this place never felt complete until we brought you here. With your help, we are going to change the world."

They knew to applaud. She gave the same speech at every party, and, though they secretly wanted to jeer and call her insane, they clapped and cheered. But Phinn knew if they kept this degree of feigned loyalty up every night, they might eventually start to believe it.

He needed to put a stop to it. He needed to get them home. With any luck, maybe Wylie was already there, waiting to greet them. He waited for the Youth Brigade to start their set and then he found Maz standing in line to get a sugar root.

"Tonight," he said to him. "Right now."

Maz nodded. Phinn stood in line with him. He was glad Nurse Conway was the one lighting the sugar roots on fire and handing them out as soon as they burst open.

"Good evening, Phinn," Nurse Conway said with disdain. He was completely devoted to Olivia, and didn't like the fact that Phinn had hurt her as a teen.

"Good evening," Phinn replied.

He watched as Nurse Conway lit a match and held it up against the bulb of the sugar root until it expanded and burst. Phinn had to act quickly. It only took the plant a few seconds to cool off enough to be eaten. Phinn grabbed the treat and pushed the bulb straight into Conway's eye.

His screams were so loud everyone could hear them over Bailey's singing. From there, it was mass chaos. Maybe Phinn had been wrong. Maybe you *could* stage a rebellion out of nowhere. He wrapped his hands around Nurse Conway's neck and started squeezing. He didn't plan to kill him, but he needed him weak and disoriented. In the distance, he could see Joshua grabbing another staff member and shoving him against the trunk of a palm tree. Bandit and Patrick fought off several orderlies that had them surrounded. Maz and Aldo held Olivia back as she screamed at them to stop, but they didn't have to listen to her anymore. *This is it*, Phinn thought. *We're going home.*

"You're going to get us out of here," Phinn said to Nurse Conway. His eye was already swollen and closing up from where the sugar root had burned him. "I will take my hands off your neck, and you will show us to the exit. Understood?"

But before Phinn could make good on his promise, he felt a wave of exhaustion rip through him. His eyes were drooping and the sounds of confusion and chaos were getting quieter.

"Today is going to be the first day of the rest of your life," Olivia had told them that morning, but it turned out it was just another day of being her hostage.

+ + + + + + +

THERE WERE WRINKLES ON HER FOREHEAD. THEY were harder to see from far away, but Olivia's face was peering at his. Phinn wasn't sure if she had tears in her eyes or if his vision was just blurry from whatever drug he was coming off of. He wanted to reach out and pull his mother's necklace off her neck, but he was afraid of how she might retaliate. He'd already asked for it back a million times, but Olivia refused to part with it. She said he'd given it to her years ago and that it technically belonged to her.

"I've tried so hard to make everyone here happy," she lamented now. "I've been so good to you. Why would you want to leave?"

Phinn looked around. He was back in his bungalow. Maz was asleep in the bed next to him.

"Are you kidding? You sound like a deluded elder," he whispered to Olivia. "You're keeping us prisoner."

"I'm taking care of you," she argued. "We had to sedate you for your own good. You'd never survive outside here on your own."

"In what universe is being here considered surviving? You're treating us like we're cadavers at a medical school."

Olivia laughed. "That's a bit dramatic."

Phinn wished he could take a time machine to the day they were on the beach and he'd discovered the gray hairs growing on Olivia's head. What if he'd said nothing? Why couldn't he have just let her stay? Lola's extended family of seventeen-year-olds had warned them about what happened to adults on the island. He thought they were only trying to make up excuses for his drug-addled parents, but maybe the island would have found its own way of getting rid of her, and none of them would be here right now.

"Let us go home, Olivia," Phinn pleaded. "You can't keep us here. You know what's going to happen. We'll turn eighteen and then we'll keep aging."

"You have nothing to worry about, toy soldier," Olivia said as she walked to the door. "Haven't you heard? Men are like fine wine. They only get better with age."

the lion's den

a loose thread from the blindfold tickled the bridge of Wylie's nose. She puffed up her cheeks and blew on it for brief respites, but the string kept landing in the same spot. She tried to pull her arms out of their restraints to adjust it, but Dr. Jay had tied thick and complicated knots that didn't allow for wiggle room. It had been hours since she'd gone to the bathroom, and they couldn't pull off at a rest spot to empty their bladders. A windowless white van, with five blindfolded kids in the back of it, wouldn't exactly make them the most inconspicuous travelers. Why did she think it was a good idea to slurp down three bowls of stew on the boat? If the drive lasted much longer, she might have to pee her pants to get some relief.

"How far are we?" she called out.

"About twenty minutes away," Dr. Jay shouted back.

"I'm going to throw up," Lola whispered next to her.

For parts of the ride, it felt like they were traveling over roads riddled with potholes. Every bump and turn sent them careening from one side of the van to the other. Lola had never ridden in a car before, and not being able to look out a window only intensified her motion sickness.

"We're almost there," Wylie told her. "But if you need to puke, you can totally puke on me."

Wylie wanted to offer more words of consolation, but she was too busy taking mental notes on their journey. At least the blindfold heightened the rest of her senses. She estimated that three hours had passed since they'd parked the boat and boarded the van. They'd been told they were traveling upstate, but that narrowed their destination to dozens of towns. An hour into the drive, the van slowed to a stop and Wylie heard the high-pitched whistle of a train barreling over rickety-sounding tracks. After they crossed the tracks, the car made a sharp left turn, and then continued driving straight for another hour until making a right turn. The bumps became more pronounced and Wylie assumed they were no longer driving along a paved road. She could hear the *ping-ping* of loose gravel hitting the windshield. There were also stretches where Dr. Jay rode the brakes as they went downhill. Aside from frequent commentary from Tinka, the group was mostly quiet during the drive. Tinka didn't seem too concerned about BioLark or their missing friends. She was just thrilled to be in a car and away from the ocean.

"This is the most fun I've had in months," Tinka announced.

"I'm gonna take a wild guess and say you don't get out much," Dr. Jay called back to her.

"I have an adventurous spirit, Doc. But I could have done without the restraints."

The blindfolds and rope were a surprise twist in Dr. Jay's plan.

"Olivia's got eyes and ears everywhere," he claimed. "It has to look like I forced you here against your will. Plus, when I started at BioLark, I signed an NDA that said I would never share the location of the facility. I'd like to avoid getting sued by my boss on top of everything else."

The paranoia reminded Wylie of a documentary her dad had made her watch with him. The film was about a cult defector who was convinced he was being watched and followed by his former leader. He slept with the lights on and kept a knife under his pillow at all times. She wondered if Dr. Jay would do that for the rest of his life, too. Back on the boat, he forbade them from discussing their plan once they reached the States.

"Someone might be listening," he'd warned them.

The cell service at the harbor was spotty, but Dr. Jay had been able to reach an old friend who was willing to bring him a van, no questions asked. They'd cut a pillowcase in strips to make the blindfolds. Hopper already had plenty of rope on the boat to tie their hands up.

"This is crazy," Micah whispered, as Wylie tied the blindfold behind his head. "If he's just using us, we're the world's biggest idiots."

Wylie thought about how her intuition had told her to trust Dr. Jay. *If Wylie Dalton thinks someone's trustworthy*, she thought wryly, *then surely they're bad news. Especially if that person is a guy.*

But she remembered the tears she'd seen fill his eyes when they'd buried his colleagues at sea, and how she'd heard him curse Olivia under his breath. His throat had constricted as he'd told them that, like most of BioLark's employees, Charlie and Kevin had no families that would miss them. But it was clear that he wouldn't forget them any time soon.

In the end, it didn't matter if Dr. Jay was lying to them. He was their only way into BioLark.

The van pulled to an abrupt stop. Wylie heard Dr. Jay turn off the ignition, unfasten his seatbelt, and slam his door shut as he stepped out of the car. A few minutes went by until he popped open the back doors.

"Get out," he ordered. His tone was cold and distant.

They slid toward the brisk air and sunlight that was pouring in. It was hard to steady themselves without using their arms for balance, but it felt good to stand and stretch their legs. Wylie could hear Lola retching her guts out.

"Sweet Jesus," Dr. Jay said. "Here, have some water."

Lola mumbled a thank you. Dr. Jay offered them each sips of water, and told them to prepare themselves for a long walk.

They must have been in a secluded place. Dr. Jay wouldn't parade around five blindfolded teenagers in a populated area. Wylie guessed they were walking through woods. Leaves crunched below her feet and she was overwhelmed by the perfume of maple syrup. Maple trees didn't actually give off a strong scent, but she'd cooked with candy cap mushrooms before, and their aroma of sugar and maple still lingered in her olfactory memory. Maybe they were in an area where the mushrooms grew. Or maybe she smelled fenugreek. She couldn't decipher the difference under duress.

When leaves and branches obstructed their way, Dr. Jay had to grab their arms and direct them, one by one. The most treacherous stretches of the hike entailed crossing streams with aggressive currents and slippery rocks. They waited patiently on the other side as Dr. Jay guided them individually over each rock. Even with full use of her arms and eyesight, Wylie would have been terrified of getting swept away by the current. It was probably better that she couldn't see the water they were crossing.

"You have to move faster," Dr. Jay yelled as Wylie briefly sat on a rock to catch her breath. The contempt in his voice was palpable. He sounded like a counselor from one of those wilderness camps for troubled youth. Wylie fumbled and her feet slipped into water up to her shins. Her socks felt like wet sponges for the rest of the trek.

"How do we know you're not going to murder us in the middle of nowhere?" Tinka asked.

"You don't," Dr. Jay replied. "Now keep it down."

"But I want to know where we are," Tinka continued to press.

"Tinka, it's okay," Micah encouraged her. "You all right, Wylie?"

"Fine, just a little damp," she called to him.

Wylie never thought she'd accept Tinka as her brother's girlfriend, but the more time she spent with them, the more she realized how good they were together. They kept each other calm in times of crisis and communicated with a brief look or gesture. Micah's bouts of anxiety had subsided and he didn't seem to rely on alcohol anymore to get him through the day. They preferred not to discuss the fact that Wylie's dad and Tinka had been involved with each other, and Wylie didn't care to remind them. Despite their unique circumstances, Micah seemed genuinely happy for the first time since he was a baby. Tinka had the ability to draw him out of his shell, and for that, Wylie would be eternally grateful. There was a time when he would have been in the throes of a panic attack right now, but instead he was the one making sure everyone else was okay.

"Stay right here," Dr. Jay snapped at them. "Don't move unless you want to get hurt."

His harsh disposition was just for show, Wylie told herself. This was part of the plan they'd agreed on together. Dr. Jay needed to make it look like they were unwilling hostages.

A high-pitched beeping sound echoed through the woods. It was followed by the click of an intercom.

"How may I assist you?" a raspy male voice asked.

"Get Olivia, *now*. Tell her Dr. Jay is here. I found five more kids on the island, and I brought them back."

"Are Dr. Porter and Dr. Cowell with you?"

"They didn't make it," Dr. Jay replied, without a trace of regret or sorrow.

After a few agonizing minutes, Wylie heard the sound of an electronic door slide open.

"Don't do anything stupid," Dr. Jay warned them, and led them inside.

As they followed him through the entrance, the air instantly felt ten degrees warmer. Oddly, it felt like the sun was beating down on them. They walked in single file down what seemed to be a narrow hallway until they were ordered to stop. Wylie heard the *ding* of an elevator, and Dr. Jay guided them inside. From the brevity of the ride, Wylie assumed they'd only gone up one floor.

Once the elevator doors opened, Dr. Jay practically pushed them out. Wylie was comforted by the scents of pineapple and coconut. Wherever they were, it smelled like vacation.

"Don't be scared," a woman's voice said. "We're not going to hurt you. We brought you here to take good care of you."

"Is that you, Olivia?" Tinka asked.

"In the flesh," Olivia answered, "though I'm a smidge more wrinkled than the last time you saw me."

Wylie's eyes popped open as someone yanked off her blindfold. The light was blinding after so many hours of darkness, but her eyes quickly adjusted as she looked around. She expected to find herself in a sterile lab or a hospital room, but they were in what appeared to be Olivia's office. The furniture looked lush and expensive, and Wylie was tempted to ask if she could lay her head down on the sofa and take a nap. The tropical smells emanated from a scented candle burning on the desk. There were framed degrees on the walls and paintings that looked like still lifes from the island.

"Phinn wasn't kidding," Olivia remarked, as she took a closer look at Wylie's face. "You're quite lovely. Your skin doesn't have a single mark on it. I remember those days fondly."

Olivia looked like she was a few years older than Wylie's parents. She was what many would describe as attractive— *for her age.* She had high cheekbones and a wide smile that looked youthful, but her eyes told a different story: puffy skin, sagging eyelids, and clumpy lashes.

"When can we see our brother?" Wylie said.

"Soon," Olivia replied. "He's a very nice kid, but so much wasted potential."

Olivia walked past Wylie to where Lola was standing, and flung her arms around her.

"I missed you, Lols," she said, using the same nickname Wylie had for her friend.

"I missed you, too," Lola answered. "I'm sorry for what Phinn did to you. I should have told you that when it happened."

"It's water under the bridge," Olivia answered. She glanced at Hopper and raised an eyebrow.

"You, I've never met," she said.

"I'm Hopper," he answered.

"What happened to your hand?" Olivia asked.

Hopper glanced at Tinka, then looked back to face Olivia.

"Phinn happened," he said.

Olivia placed her hand on top of his head and mussed his curls. "We're glad to have you here," she told him.

The kids sat quietly as Dr. Jay described finding Micah and Tinka on the island, while leaving out the fact that they saved him from sinking into quicksand. The rest of the kids, he told Olivia, had arrived by boat. She seemed to well up when he revealed the fate of their colleagues, though she didn't pretend to be surprised by the news.

"I'm glad you made it out alive, sweetie," she said, planting a kiss on Dr. Jay's forehead.

Their affection for each other alarmed Wylie. Back on the island, Dr. Jay merely described Olivia as an eccentric woman who signed his paychecks, but the ease in their rapport suggested a closer bond.

"I want you to write a full report on your findings. I'll get our guests acclimated."

None of them said anything as Dr. Jay left the office. They weren't supposed to like him. They needed to seem afraid of him. But Wylie expected a subtle look or nod that indicated he was still on their side. Nothing.

"You must be exhausted," Olivia said, with a tone of maternal concern. "And you're probably wondering why you're here."

"Not really," Tinka piped in. "I'm pretty sure it has something to do with an extravagant revenge plot. You're really selling that whole 'mad scientist' vibe with the lab coat."

"This has nothing to do with revenge. It's about sharing the gifts of Minor Island with the rest of the world. And you're here to help me do that."

As if on cue, the elevator doors opened and a man in scrubs stepped into the room. He had bruises on his neck and wore a patch over his right eye. He didn't speak to them as he used a knife to cut through their ropes, but Wylie's hackles rose when she felt his hand on her arm.

"I always felt so bad for you," Tinka said to Olivia, as the man worked to loosen her restraints. "I remember the day you were exiled. I've never seen anyone cry that hard. I was glad you were leaving, but I've wondered about you since. How does anyone move on from something like that? Now I know the answer: they don't."

Olivia smiled warmly in response. "You know, if you weren't so petite and porcelain, you wouldn't get away with that attitude. We'll have to work on that. Anyway, let's get you showered and fed and properly medicated."

They shifted nervously as Olivia opened a wooden box on her desk and removed a handful of *rahat* flowers that were smaller and paler in hue than the crop that grew on the island.

"We're growing these ourselves now. They're genetically modified, but they still have the intended effect."

Olivia told them to swallow an entire flower each, insisting that they didn't pack as much of a punch as the ones back home. Wylie had tried *rahat* for the first time a few nights before, and Hopper had told her that a single petal would lull her right to sleep. She'd followed his advice and within minutes, her eyelids collapsed and she was consumed by a deep slumber. Ingesting an entire flower seemed like it would have the power to shut down her organs and kill her, but it didn't appear that taking the drug was optional. Maybe it would help quiet Wylie's nerves. She was eager to see Joshua, but she would also be forced to see Phinn again.

After they each swallowed a flower, Olivia and the man in the scrubs led them toward a locker room to get cleaned up. The hallways reminded Wylie of a hospital, minus the gurneys and beeping monitors and frantic visitors.

The steaming shower made the entire trip worth it. Wylie almost didn't care what they did to her now. She stood completely still as the hot water spilled over her skin, wiping off the dirt and grime she'd accrued on the hike through the woods. The effects of the *rahat* flowers crept up on her slowly. They steadied her thoughts, but they also made her feel like she could do anything. It had been a long time since she'd drunk alcohol, but she recognized the sensation of total confidence. The future was wide open with possibilities. Finding their way to BioLark was half the battle. Now they just had to get out. It didn't even matter that a mousy female nurse stood guard behind the stall doors as she finished showering. What mattered was that the towels here were fluffy and soft and warm.

As she dried off, the nurse wordlessly handed her a pair of hospital scrubs. The fabric was stiff and the style was plain, aside from a pocket square on the shirt with the emblem of a bird trapped inside a test tube. Wylie dutifully put on the uniform. It was too soon to be disobedient. They needed to heed Dr. Jay's advice. The more they cooperated, the more surprised Olivia would be when they fought their way out.

After she got dressed, Wylie was escorted into what looked like an employee lounge and was told to help herself to a plate of sandwiches and a cooler filled with soda and bottled water. Hopper and Tinka were the only two present, and they were quietly eating their sandwiches. Until now, the two had kept as much distance from each other as possible. She knew Tinka was desperate to apologize for what she'd done to Hopper, but that she didn't know where to start.

Micah and Lola arrived at the same time, and they scarfed down the food that was offered to them. Even Lola had her appetite back. The fare was simple, but they were too hungry to care. By the time Olivia arrived, there was nothing left to eat or drink.

"How is everyone feeling?" Olivia inquired.

"Good," Wylie managed to say, but the drowsiness was setting in.

"It's not bedtime yet," Olivia warned. "I have a surprise for you. You're going to want to stay awake for this."

Hopper took Wylie's hand as they walked out the door and she squeezed his back.

"How do you feel, Hops?" she asked. "You're moments from seeing Nadia. You want to practice your opening line on me?"

Hopper laughed and shook his head.

"Dalton," he whispered. "You're gonna break my good fingers if you don't loosen your grip."

Wylie softened her hold, but didn't let go.

She was so tangled up in her thoughts that she nearly didn't notice the linoleum floors had turned into plastic planks of wood. The neon-lit hallways had disappeared behind them, and it no longer felt like they were indoors. The temperature reminded her of warm summer nights in the city where restaurant patios filled up with New Yorkers who forgot winter had ever existed. She looked up and discovered a dome shaped sky that was the color of black nail polish. Every inch of it was covered in tiny stars that glittered more brightly than the ones that danced over the *parvaz* field.

"It looks like home," Tinka said.

Wylie looked around to see rows of bungalows on either side of them. She heard music playing, and she could swear it was Bailey's voice traveling through her ear canal.

"You built this place?" Lola asked. She was walking alongside Olivia.

"I did. Isn't it glorious?"

"Not as glorious as the real thing," Tinka muttered.

Olivia ignored the comment and led them through a narrow opening between bungalows that gave way to a staircase.

"Welcome to your residency party," she announced.

Wylie gazed at what looked like an architect's mock-up of the Clearing. It felt like someone had decided to perform a school play about the island, and this was the set they'd built. She instinctively squeezed Hopper's hand, careful not to hurt him this time. She knew they were both anxious about finding Phinn among the crowd of kids below them. But they had each other and they could conquer the fear together.

two truths and no lies

they were no longer allowed to have sugar roots at the evening soirees Olivia forced them to attend. She announced the new rule during breakfast, and told everyone they could blame Phinn.

"He ruined it for all of you," she said. "I know. He's *such* an elder."

Normally, Phinn wouldn't have cared, but no one liked the food here and the sugar roots were a nice reminder of where they came from. He liked to eat them with his eyes closed, so that he could make believe that they were back home, and not in some fake version of the Clearing. He thought about taking a dip in the lagoon to clear his head, but the smell of chlorine made it less appealing.

He was officially depressed. They'd tried to escape, but it hadn't worked. Perhaps it was poor planning on their part, but they didn't have the luxury of mobilizing an army when Nurse Conway and others like him eavesdropped on their every word.

"We have company!" Olivia's voice bellowed through the room.

He turned toward Olivia's voice, expecting to see an influx of staff members to keep them in line, but instead, there were five kids standing next to her. The drugs made everything look blurry in the distance, but Phinn could swear one of the kids looked like Tinka. He pushed his way through the small crowd so that he could get a closer look.

It worked, he thought. The universe had finally rewarded him for his penance. Wylie had returned to him.

"*Wylie!*" he cried at the top of his lungs.

He saw a look of discomfort cross her face. From there, every other discovery seemed to fast-forward. There was a boy standing next to her—a clean-cut version of Hopper. There was a girl standing on the other side. It was *Lola*. Phinn felt his heart drop into his stomach and dissolve. He wanted to run, but there was nowhere to go. It was time for his final reckoning.

He hung back as he watched Micah and Wylie run to Joshua. Even when Phinn and Wylie had supposedly been in love, she'd always put her brothers first. The Daltons embraced in a group hug, and held on for dear life.

His eyes darted away from them to Lola and Maz. They took a few tentative steps toward each other, and then Maz sprinted up the staircase and met her halfway. Lola flung her arms around him and it seemed like they melded into one person as they held each other. Phinn couldn't hear what they whispered to one another before they dove into passionate kisses in the middle of the staircase. *Love really does conquer all*, Phinn thought as they either refused to come up for air or didn't need to breathe in each other's presence.

"Poor Phinn," he heard a girl's voice say. "He has no one to run to."

He'd been so focused on the others that he hadn't even noticed Tinka now standing beside him. She let her hand rest on his shoulder. There was a time when Phinn would have removed it or called her impossibly clingy, but right now, he was glad to feel the featherweight of her palm on his body.

"Can I hug you?' he asked.

"Fine," Tinka said. But as they embraced, she whispered, "I know what you did to Lola."

"And check it out," she added as they separated. "You're the reason they're still scared of the poor guy."

Hopper was awkwardly milling around next to the Dalton siblings. Phinn had never expected to see him again. He certainly never expected to see him with Wylie. It had taken the other kids a minute to recognize him without his beard and long hair, but once they spotted the three missing fingers on his right hand, they retreated in fear. Phinn could see the embarrassment on Hopper's face, but he wasn't sure if it was from being treated like a social pariah or from witnessing firsthand that no one was more important to Wylie than her brothers.

"He's dangerous!" Nadia screamed to one of the BioLark employees. "You need to get him out of here. He's *not* one of us."

The outburst forced Lola and Maz to break apart.

"He is one of us," Lola said firmly.

Lola didn't have to be loud or combative to capture everyone's attention. Though he'd never admit it to anyone, Phinn had never been afraid that his power would be usurped by any of the guys on the island. Lola was the only person he worried would make a better leader than him. It was a mystery to him why no one else had realized that yet. Now she addressed the kids.

"Phinn made you believe that Hopper kidnapped me, but that's not what happened," she said.

Phinn didn't know where to focus. If he looked down at his feet, he would appear sheepish at best, and pathetic at worst. But he couldn't bear to see the disgust on Wylie's face or the smug satisfaction on Olivia's. Most of all, he didn't want to watch Maz process the fact that he'd been a loyal soldier to a guy who'd stripped him of the person he loved most in the world.

"What's she talking about, Phinn?" Maz asked.

"I made a mistake," was the only thing Phinn could utter.

He had enough *parvaz* left in his system to breeze off and let them sort out the details on their own. He didn't need to be here for this. But where would he fly? He would have to meander in circles above them, a shark without teeth.

Instead, he stood there and listened, full of shame, as Lola described to everyone the day she learned the truth about Gregory Dalton and confronted Phinn on his boat. Her voice never wavered as she recounted what it felt like to drift alone in the ocean on a raft, certain she was going to die and that no one would find out what really happened to her. But Hopper had come along and rescued her. He'd rescued Wylie, too.

The kids turned to Phinn—some incredulous, some furious. He couldn't look Maz in the eye to see what his best friend was feeling.

"It's true," he confessed. "It's all true."

* * * * * * *

FOR WEEKS, WYLIE HAD DREADED THE IDEA OF SEEING Phinn again. What if, after everything, she still found herself drawn to him? What if she still found him attractive and charismatic? What would that make her—an addicted girlfriend? A bad feminist? A needy human?

But none of those emotions resurfaced when she set eyes on his scrambled teeth and amber hair and broad shoulders. She didn't feel an inkling of sympathy or pity. He was someone she didn't want in her life anymore. Wylie wanted him to melt away from the amusement park version of the Clearing they were standing in.

"It's true," Phinn muttered. "It's all true."

At least he was done making excuses for himself. The others were only now discovering the true low of Phinn's wrongdoings. But Wylie had her own truths to reconfigure. Here she was, back with her brother. Joshua's hair was trimmed short and there were no signs of stubble on his face. He looked surprisingly healthy and well rested. His eyes had turned into puddles at the sight of Wylie, and she could hear him crying as they hugged. All this time, he'd probably assumed she was dead.

"I'm sorry," he kept repeating over and over again, but she didn't know what he had to apologize for.

She wanted to reassure him that they had a plan to get him out of here, but Dr. Jay had warned them that the place was bugged. Instead, Wylie hugged him back and told him that everything was going to be okay. She kept her arm around him while Lola confessed Phinn's sins for him. Joshua had trusted Phinn even when Wylie had stopped. She knew it wouldn't be easy to hear that he was worse than they all thought.

"Well, this has been a fascinating window into the collapse of a leader," Olivia broke in. "Lola, you're a survivor. You're safe with us. We won't let Phinn hurt you again."

It felt odd to go through such a personal encounter in the presence of virtual strangers employed by BioLark. This was not the showdown they'd expected those nights on Hopper's boat. They were supposed to make these revelations in the *real* Clearing, not one put together with purchases from the garden section of a Home Depot.

"You left her there to *die*?" Maz asked Phinn, ignoring everyone else around them.

"I didn't want her to die," Phinn replied. "I just needed to make it go away."

"So you could be with Wylie." Maz didn't phrase it as a question.

Wylie felt sickened that she was the motive for the crimes against Lola. She remembered the nights she and Phinn stayed up late in bed, speculating about her best friend's disappearance. Wylie had even suggested that Maz might be guilty of getting rid of Lola. It was a ridiculous theory.

Especially since the person responsible had been sleeping next to her all along.

Wylie expected Maz to hurl punches at Phinn. Instead, Maz only embraced Lola tighter. It was no easy feat to direct your energy on the person you loved instead of the person you hated. But Maz was better than most people.

"You hurt people, Phinn," Hopper finally spoke up. "It's the only thing you're good at."

"I have a lot of regrets," Phinn admitted. "But I don't regret what I did to you."

Wylie watched as Hopper threw his whole body at Phinn and repeatedly punched him with both fists. A mist of blood sprayed from Phinn's face and the BioLark staff finally intervened and pulled Hopper away. Wylie half expected to see Aldo and Patrick rush to his side and tend to his wounds, but they didn't go near him.

"I guess we'll have to keep you two separated," Olivia declared. "Let's call it a night and see how we all feel in the morning. I'll show you to your bungalows."

Space was limited in the bungalows, which meant Olivia had to reconsider their sleeping arrangements. Maz didn't want to be anywhere near Phinn, so he was given a room to share with Lola. When it became clear that the Daltons wanted to stick together, Tinka volunteered to take one for the team and room with Phinn. At first, Wylie expected Micah to succumb to a panic attack, but he wasn't the least bit concerned.

"I trust her," he told Wylie.

Hopper was the only one left without a place to sleep, but Bandit stepped forward and offered his room.

"It's the least I can do after everything we put you through," Bandit said.

The Daltons' bungalow had two bunk beds and a single bed. Wylie pulled rank as the oldest and called dibs on the single bed. Joshua and Micah arm-wrestled for the top bunk and Joshua won. It all felt so normal. Wylie wanted to ask Joshua what they could expect from this place, but he seemed so relaxed and happy that she didn't want to spoil the moment. They could make believe they were in Montauk, huddled in their vacation home, complaining and comparing notes about all the annoying things their parents had done that day.

It felt weird to lie back in bed and look up at a ceiling made of plaster and paint. Wylie instantly felt claustrophobic not getting to see stars like on Hopper's boat or the palm fronds of the island.

"It's awful here," Joshua whispered once the lights were off.

"I can't wait to go home," Micah said.

"Where is home?" Wylie asked.

"The island," Micah replied. "And not the one with the crowded subway stations and monster skyscrapers and parents who make each other unhappy."

Joshua rolled onto his side and mumbled:

"Home doesn't exist anymore."

the next generation

the first few days at BioLark were surprisingly bearable. Wylie smiled through the tests and drug trials, and expertly played the role of resident optimist. No silver linings went undetected and no glasses were half empty in her presence. She would have gladly tap danced and broken out in song if she thought it would get Joshua, or anyone else, out of their funk.

But by day four, something shifted. As her mood began to nosedive, bright sides and pep talks became a ludicrous notion. It could have been the heavy dose of medication or the slow death of her taste buds, but once day fourteen rolled around, Wylie officially displayed all the symptoms of a deep depression.

It didn't help that Dr. Jay had essentially ghosted them. *He was real*, she had to remind herself. Dr. Jay wasn't a figment of Wylie's imagination. He was the person who made good on his promise to take them to BioLark. Wylie had to mentally recount these details and facts every day. Between the pills, the regimented flights, the hormone injections, and the nurses walking into their bungalow at all hours of the night to draw blood and record their temperatures, it was getting harder to remember who was who and what was what.

"You remember Dr. Jay, right?" she asked Micah each morning.

"Yes, Wylie. I remember him. You're not going crazy."

Then where the hell was he? Two weeks had gone by since he'd guided them through the maple-scented woods and into the lion's den. He'd never warned them that he'd disappear once they were posing as patients. They'd been told they'd see him every day. He was supposed to find access to the tunnels that would set them free and get them home.

Unless it was all a ruse. Dr. Jay just needed to escape an island that wanted him dead and he manipulated the kids into bringing him here. Wylie had led her friends astray. The worst thing anyone, including her, could do was trust her judgment.

"How are you feeling today, Dalton?" Hopper asked, as she took a seat across from him at breakfast.

Terrible, lost, alone, angry, tired, defeated, scared, anxious.

"I feel fine, Hops," Wylie answered.

Lately, she'd been preoccupied with the memory of the night Phinn first took her to the *parvaz* field. She remembered how the lush scenery and salty air made her feel brave enough to open up to him about the accident in the Hamptons. As they sat beneath the willow tree together, she was overwhelmed by Phinn's support. He'd known her at her worst, and he didn't bolt.

But she'd been wrong about the first part of that equation. Aside from that night, Phinn had always seen Wylie at her best. In the early days on the island, she was brimming with joy. She took pleasure in cooking food and tending to the garden. She stared at every new herb and plant with unadulterated wonder. She kissed passionately and forgave easily. Ignorance was truly bliss.

It was Hopper who'd seen Wylie at her worst. She didn't smile as much anymore. She was irritable and short-tempered and tired all the time. The foods here made her stomach expand and constrict in ways that made her think her insides were riddled with ulcers. The sheer sight of the nurses and orderlies made her blood pressure rise like mercury measuring a fever. Every morning she woke up wondering if the burns and cuts on her back would ever heal. According to Olivia, drug trials took years to complete, and they still hadn't figured out what kept Minor Island residents in a permanent state of teenhood. Every day they were here was another day closer to their eighteenth birthdays. Before long, living on the island wouldn't even be an option.

"You don't seem fine," Hopper said, taking a bite of his processed cereal.

He chose his words carefully these days. Hopper knew from experience that one wrong comment could set Wylie off. Sometimes Wylie felt smothered by the pressure to be okay around him. The guy who'd been stoic and withdrawn when they'd met was now the keeper of perspective.

"Just remember that we've been through worse," he pointed out.

Wylie wasn't so sure. She'd rather be in a jail cell on the island than trapped in a prison by someone who pretended she was using them to make the world a better place. And she couldn't say a word about it. At BioLark, the punishment always far outweighed the crime. Maybe they'd wean her off *rahat* flowers so she could feel every pinprick and razor's edge during the pain tests. Or they'd double the dose of *parvaz* and force her to fly for twenty-four hours without breaks. So Wylie's hateful tirades remained where they were safe: inside her head. It was the only place BioLark couldn't listen.

Olivia Weckler is a sad old lady who will die alone.

That particular mantra helped her survive the "therapy" appointments with Olivia. Sometimes she used variations on the same theme. *Olivia is a sad old lady whom no one loves. Olivia is a sad old lady who has no life.* If she repeated the mantras over and over again, it was much easier to bite her tongue for the entirety of the session.

"It's impolite not to talk, Wylie," Olivia would scold. "I helped your dad get his life together on the mainland. If it weren't for me, you wouldn't even have been born."

It was strange putting the true pieces of her dad's life together. Between Olivia's stories and the anecdotes her friends shared from the island, Wylie realized that she'd been raised by a stranger. She was impressed with her dad, though. He could have turned out like Dr. Weckler, but Gregory had managed the impossible. He'd lived on the island, left on his own accord, and then moved on with his life.

"Are you even listening to me, Dalton?" Hopper asked, waving a hand in her face. "Are you gonna be okay today?"

"I'll be fine once I have some *parvaz* in my system," was the most cordial response she could give.

The daily flights were the only part of the days at BioLark that Wylie looked forward to. Some hated being dosed with *parvaz* for such a long period of time, but Wylie used the opportunity to clear her muddled mind. It was good exercise to kick her legs and flap her arms. The muscles in her body were getting firm and it was nice to know she was strong on the outside when she felt so weak on the inside. The natural endorphins were probably keeping her alive. She hated that Nurse Conway slowed her down every thirty minutes to take her pulse and swab the sweat off her forehead. But today the interruption gave Lola a chance to catch up to her.

"I need to talk to you," Lola said. "But you have to slow down."

"What's wrong?" Wylie asked.

Lola's chin quivered and her shoulders collapsed in heavy sobs.

"I thought I was fine until you asked me what was wrong," she said.

They weren't allowed to take breaks, but Wylie didn't care. She held on to Lola's hand and they perched themselves at the top of a plastic palm tree. It swayed under their weight, not as sturdy as the real thing. A cool breeze swept over them. Wylie thought the wind was picking up until she spotted a fan oscillating on the wall.

"Dr. Weckler showed me the results of my blood work," Lola said.

What was wrong with the universe? If Wylie was about to find out that her best friend was terminally ill, she would lose the little faith she had left in the world. Lola leaned in and whispered:

"*I'm pregnant.*"

"How?" Wylie asked.

Lola confessed that the pregnancy wasn't an accident and that she was four months along. She'd been puking for months after every birth control ritual to remove the pill from her system. It was Maz who'd first brought up the idea of a baby, but she'd quickly agreed it was something she wanted to do. Lola hated the idea of her tribe dying out with her, but beyond that, she had *wanted* to get exiled. Eager to discover life on the mainland, she'd seen a pregnancy as the perfect exit strategy.

"Now that I'm here, though," Lola said, "All I want is to have this baby back home. I won't let Olivia treat my pregnancy like a science experiment. I want my kid to have a childhood like the one I did, filled with doggy paddles in the lagoon and somersaults in midair. I want my baby to grow up on the *real* island, and not in a place where they'll be treated like some freak of nature."

Lola's eyes lit up when she talked about having a child. Wylie tried to offer words of encouragement, but she didn't know the first thing about motherhood. Lola seemed so much older and more sophisticated than Wylie now. And she was. They may have looked the same age, but Lola had been on this earth for far longer.

Wylie tried to imagine what she would be like as a mom. The island was its own corner of paradise, but like Lola, she liked to think her future progeny could share her childhood experiences. The Christmas tree at Rockefeller Center, frozen hot chocolates at Serendipity, and snow angels on ski trips topped the list.

"Olivia said I'll be able to feel the baby move in a couple weeks. I already feel so protective. I already feel like I can't live without this creature growing inside me."

Wylie's mom had made a similar comment once. It was after their parents announced they were getting divorced and Micah and Wylie had to decide which parent they wanted to live with. Joshua used to joke that he was the lucky one who got to go to juvie. One night, when Wylie had stayed up way too late baking cookies for her basketball team, Maura simply looked at her and said: "I can't live without you." But Wylie couldn't tell if the admission was motivated by unconditional love or if Maura just wanted to win.

"Can I touch it?" Wylie asked. Lola nodded and placed Wylie's hands on her abdomen. She could feel Lola's formerly innie belly button poking out through her shirt. Her stomach was more taut than Wylie expected, and had protruded into the size of a volleyball. If their scrubs were more fitted, than everyone would have noticed the pregnancy.

"I hope it's a girl," Lola said.

"Me too," Wylie answered.

Olivia wanted to find a way to make people young again.

She wanted to find a way to make *herself* young again. The teenagers in her care didn't seem to be providing any leads on that front. The island was too dangerous to explore. But a baby was a game changer. Especially one with the blood of a Minor Island native. The pregnancy was a blessing for Maz and Lola, but it was also a windfall for BioLark.

They could no longer bide their time for Dr. Jay to return, Wylie realized. They'd have to find the tunnels on their own. Before Wylie took her palms off Lola's belly, she made a silent promise to the baby growing inside:

I'm going to get you home safe and sound, little one.

suicide watch

phinn was happy today. Euphoric, even. Nothing would bother him. When Nurse Conway banged on the door and ordered him and Tinka to get up for breakfast, he leapt out of bed. He was excited to feast on his bowl of instant oatmeal without being forced to make conversation with anyone. If he got changed quickly enough, he'd even get to see the fake sunrise on his way to the dining hall. This time, when Tinka declared that it was "day fifteen of the *Everyone Wants Phinn to Die* show," he was able to laugh off the comment. The dig had previously left him feeling forlorn, but today, it was hilarious. Especially the way Tinka made a fist and pretended to blow into a trumpet before she said it.

"You're laughing," Tinka observed.

"I am!" Phinn replied. "It's funny, because it's true."

He changed into a fresh pair of scrubs with no concern

that Tinka could see him naked. Modesty was unnecessary in her presence. Especially not today of all days.

"Thanks, Tinka," he said before leaving the bungalow.

"For what?" she asked.

"For being such a good friend to me."

"We're not friends, Phinn."

"We were for fifty years or so."

The orange juice tasted different at breakfast. Phinn concentrated on the tart flavor as it pierced his taste buds and trickled down his throat. So what if it wasn't freshly squeezed? It came in adorable little cartons and raised his blood sugar to a comfortable level. He didn't mind that at the other tables, the kids were whispering among themselves. For once, he didn't look down at his bowl of oatmeal like it was the most fascinating display of grain he'd ever seen. He looked right at his former friends. There was plenty of misery to go around. The smiles among them were forced and half-hearted. Bandit especially looked withdrawn and sad this morning.

Despite their predicament, Phinn could hear them trying to keep each other's spirits up by recounting stories from the island. On this particular morning, Wylie's laughter rang out louder than anyone else's. It had been a long time since Phinn had heard it. If Phinn could put the sound of her laugh on a loop and listen to it all day, he would. He watched as she giggled and simultaneously cringed at a story Maz shared from when her dad lived on the island. Phinn privately smiled at the memory. They'd been at Olivia's residency party when an intoxicated Gregory had decided to strip off his clothes and fly in the nude. Phinn nearly interjected when Maz left out the most important detail of the night. Gregory needed to take a piss, but didn't have enough time to land before he relieved himself. The party had abruptly ended with several kids jumping in the lagoon to rinse urine out of their hair. It was too bad Wylie would never hear that part of the story.

Phinn only got to observe Wylie's behavior from a distance, but this morning, she seemed like she'd turned a corner in her depression. Phinn noticed a goofy grin on Hopper's face at the sight of Wylie's smile. He recognized the twinkle in Hopper's eye, the flush of his cheeks, and the way he kept staring when Wylie was no longer paying attention to him. He was in love. Who could blame him? Phinn certainly couldn't.

When they waited in line for the day's cocktail of drugs, Phinn didn't gag as he placed the flowers—now in pill form—on his tongue. He didn't ask Nurse Conway how he was able to live with himself. He didn't even spit the pills across the room. Instead, he smiled as he swallowed them and graciously thanked Olivia for keeping them properly medicated.

"Drugs are tropic!" he declared, raising both of his arms in the air.

The comment was either met with silent glares or vocal insults. But neither came from Maz. His best friend had mastered the art of pretending Phinn didn't exist. Soon, that would be even easier.

For Phinn, the hours of flying between the plastic shrubbery and the planetarium-like sky felt much shorter than usual. *Time flies when you're running out of it*, Phinn thought to himself. He didn't even complain as an orderly hooked him up to a heart monitor and a nurse used electrical currents to test his pain threshold. Nothing would hurt today. Not even Olivia's tired line of questioning.

"How did your parents kill themselves, Phinn?" Olivia asked, like she always did in their evening therapy session. The question had been framed a hundred different ways, but Phinn never had the will to answer.

"Adults are supposed to be reliable, aren't they?" she goaded. "*Parents* are supposed to be reliable."

Phinn nodded. Olivia had been brought into the world by wealthy socialites who paraded her around at parties but otherwise ignored her presence. Even as children, Phinn and Olivia had known that adults failed at being wiser than them. That their parents didn't shield them from ugly truths that would eventually reveal themselves as they grew older. Truths like the fact that dreams weren't always realized. That your every whim would be ruled by the balance of your bank account. And that people you loved wouldn't always love you back, and even when they did, they could still die.

But he replied to the question the same way he did every day.

"No comment, Dr. Weckler."

The death of his parents was a story he would take to his grave. After tonight, she could badger Maz and Tinka for the answer. Now the only thing left to do was tie up loose ends with Lola, and then, like his mom and dad, he could slip away forever.

Phinn had spent many nights staying awake until the drugs wore off, mulling over ways to set the kids free and get them back to the island in one piece. But eventually he decided there was no plan he could carry out without the cooperation of others. It was time to give up.

Suffering through yet another party in the Clearing wasn't so rough when you knew it was going to be your last. His plan was so simple, it was a mystery why he hadn't come up with it before. None of the BioLark staff had a proper view of anything that took place on behind the waterfall in the lagoon. They'd have to stand guard next to it to regulate any activity in its vicinity. He'd seen Micah and Tinka sneak off with each other each night to make out, but they always waited a half hour before they casually broke off from the group. It made him sad that Tinka would have to be the one to discover his body.

In an homage to his parents, Phinn would stand in the lagoon and swallow the *rahat* pills he'd been hoarding for the past two weeks. Luckily for him, the nurse who administered the kids' nightly dose wasn't thorough about making sure they were properly swallowed.

It wouldn't take long for him to fall asleep and drown in the shallow water of the lagoon. He should have died in the ocean the night that Wylie left him. It would be a fitting end to his story.

Lola might have been more receptive to talking to him if she knew he was minutes from death, but Phinn didn't want to tell her what he was planning.

"It won't take long," he begged. "It's about the island."

"Leave us alone," Maz snapped.

"No," Phinn said, standing his ground.

"I'll only be a minute, okay?" Lola relented. Maz glowered, but she told him, "The last thing we need right now is one of those orderlies going crazy with a Taser because you two start punching each other."

Phinn led Lola toward the lagoon, and away from the rest of the kids.

"You need to replace me," he said as soon as they were alone.

"What do you mean, 'replace' you?" Lola asked.

"If you get back to the island, you'll need a new leader."

Lola remained poised. "Last time I checked, you didn't get a say anymore."

"You're the only native resident," Phinn pointed out stubbornly. "You have the skills and the disposition to be the greatest leader the place has had. And that says a lot coming from someone with my ego."

Lola shook her head. "The future of Minor Island doesn't involve you."

"*Exactly*," Phinn said.

Lola let out a frustrated breath. "Look, not that it's any of your concern, but we already voted. Maz will be in charge of the island and I couldn't be happier."

Tinka had told Phinn as much. It was infuriating that the other kids hadn't come to the same conclusion as him. He didn't bother extolling Lola's virtues or listing off the bevy of reasons she was qualified for the job. He considered it an insult to tell her everything she already knew to be true about herself. Plus, he didn't have the time.

"Who would cook the meals?" she asked.

"Wylie. Someone, anyone. You can even train Maz to do it. You'll figure it out. You make some mean chipney onion cakes, but the island can live without them."

"It's not that simple anymore," Lola said. She looked close to tears. And then, without her knowing they'd be the last words he'd ever hear: "You were my friend, Phinn. You left me on a boat to *die*."

Phinn's guilt overcame him. It must have seemed preposterous to be giving her advice, but he needed to get his affairs in order and do what was best for the island.

"I'm sorry," Phinn said. "And you can ignore me all you want, but you know I'm right about this," he said before Lola walked away without a response. He watched her return to Maz. The questioning look of anger on his former best friend's face told him it was time.

Four of the *rahat* pills were easily swallowed down without water, but Phinn needed to cup fluid from the lagoon to take the rest. He walked toward the waterfall where no one would be able to see him, and turned back to get one last look at Wylie. She wasn't smiling anymore. The same vacant look he'd gotten used to had repossessed her face. He was mad at himself for looking at her. He wanted to remember the girl who beamed the first time he gave her *parvaz* and they soared through the sky above Brooklyn together.

Before he could close his eyes and focus his mind on that image, he noticed Bandit standing on the deck above the Clearing. Phinn watched as Bandit flung one leg over the railing and looked out at his friends. Phinn was instantly consumed with dread. He sloshed his way through the water, and stepped out of the lagoon, as Bandit placed a finger in his mouth and whistled loudly to get everyone's attention.

"Guess what today is?" he yelled. "It's my eighteenth birthday, and no one here got me a cake."

Phinn knew what was going to happen before anyone else seemed to. Phinn had forgotten that Bandit was barely a month shy of becoming an adult when he whisked him to the island. His time was up. He wouldn't get to return home and stay young forever. The deck was high enough that if Bandit jumped off, he would be dead from the impact of hitting the ground.

Phinn refused to outlive Bandit.

Phinn flew toward the deck.

Bandit jumped.

Phinn caught him.

He was kicking and screaming at Phinn to let him go by the time they landed on the ground.

"I didn't want to be saved!" he screamed. "I wanted to die! My life is over anyway."

Phinn pressed his arms down in an effort to soothe him. The kids were already surrounding them.

"Your life isn't over," Phinn told him, practically yelling to make himself heard. "You're going to see your mom again. She's clean and sober now. She spends every day walking around the city, putting up flyers with your picture on them. You'll go home to her, and you'll get to grow up. You'll meet someone and fall in love and get married and have kids who think their dad hung the stars and moon. And you'll tell them bedtime stories about the island. Your life isn't over, Bandit. It's just beginning."

The BioLark orderlies pulled Phinn off of Bandit before he could respond. Olivia mumbled something about placing him on suicide watch, and the staff dragged him away.

To everyone else, it looked like Phinn had saved Bandit's life, but it was the other way around. Phinn was supposed to be sinking in the lagoon right now. The few *rahat* pills he'd taken made him feel groggy, but the high dose of *parvaz* from this morning still hadn't worn off. Phinn allowed his body to rise up to the ceiling. He watched as the kids below him shrank in size. From his vantage point, he could no longer tell if they were looking at him like a hero or a traitor.

It didn't matter either way. He didn't break Bandit's fall to win friends or regain his popularity. He did it because the world needed Bandit in it. Death wasn't better than old age. And now he was still alive, too.

As Phinn did a back flip in the sky, he felt something tumble out of his pocket and rain down on the Clearing. It was the ten leftover *rahat* pills he'd worked so hard to save. But he didn't feel like he needed them anymore.

Your life isn't over, he told himself. *It's just beginning.*

punchbowl

they stared at each other across the table like they did every day. Wylie's thoughts, whirling around her head like cars stuck at a rotary, barred her from repeating her mantras. She liked to go blank during the therapy sessions with Olivia, but lately, that was impossible. Lola was pregnant. Over the past few days, her belly had protruded into the shape of an igloo, making the pregnancy common knowledge. Maz spent most of his free time with his hand pressed against her belly, hoping the baby would greet him with a kick and give them a sign that everything was going to be okay. The rest of the kids, through their haze of pills and clinical depression, didn't know whether to be happy for Lola or upset. Phinn's rules were still ingrained in them, and some couldn't reconcile the pregnancy with the oath they'd taken *never* to reproduce. But most of the girls, Wylie included, thought Lola was a hero for doing what she wanted with her body.

"Are you going to take Lola's baby away from her?" Wylie asked Olivia.

"Wow. She actually speaks," Olivia replied.

"Answer me. Are you ever going to let us go?"

Olivia nodded. "Eventually. You've been kept from your families for long enough. I look forward to the day when I can return you to them. I know your dad will be especially grateful. He'd hate the idea of Phinn being responsible for your disappearance."

"I don't like being here with Phinn," Wylie confessed. "It makes me uncomfortable."

She didn't know why the words came out of her mouth, but it felt good to say them.

"Why?" Olivia asked.

"Because . . . I used to love him. And seeing him every day reminds me how naïve I was. How easily I can fall for someone just because they shower me with compliments and call me 'porcelain.' I don't like feeling that way."

Olivia leaned back in her seat and gave Wylie a smile that wasn't part of her usual repertoire. It wasn't condescending or manic or vindictive. It almost seemed sympathetic.

"No one does," Olivia said. "At least you broke up with him. You were the one who walked away. I got dumped and tossed on a boat. He told me I was going to be too old for him. He was right."

"How did you get over it?"

Wylie wasn't sure what she was doing. Why was it suddenly so easy to open up to this woman?

"I threw myself into work. Medical school helped. I was

so busy I didn't have enough time to think about him. I don't know what hurt more: losing him or not being allowed to live on the island."

Wylie realized Olivia had no one else she could talk to about these things either. Gregory had shut her out of his life. She probably didn't have any girlfriends she could grab martinis with and wax poetic about that seventeen-year-old boy who kicked her off a tropical island where no one got older.

"Is all of this your revenge, then?" Wylie asked.

Olivia shook her head. "I didn't want my pain to be for nothing. I want to help people. The medical advancements we could make here are unprecedented. We're doing important work."

The monitor started to beep loudly. Wylie's heart rate had gone up. She'd nearly lost count of how many days remained before she turned eighteen. Who would she be if she never returned to Minor Island? In one corner, there was Olivia, a woman so preoccupied with her youth that she'd spent her entire fortune trying to reclaim it. In the other corner stood her dad, a man who had to bury his past in order to function. They'd both lost a piece of themselves in the process.

"Phinn said once that I was beyond compare," Olivia confessed. "How do you say that to someone and then send them away?"

Wylie didn't have the heart to tell her that "beyond compare" was his favorite compliment, and one he'd given to Wylie and Tinka and probably a dozen other girls. It meant absolutely nothing. She didn't mention that she'd also worn the tiny mirror that was now strung around Olivia's neck. Phinn's family heirloom had made the rounds.

"After you left, did you ever meet anyone else you cared about as much?" Wylie asked, genuinely curious.

Olivia shook her head. "Love is never forever. Love has a finite conclusion. Whether it's death or divorce or boredom, there is always going to be pain at the end. I never wanted to feel that way again."

There was something about Olivia that Wylie recognized in herself. The way she'd taken her hurt and made a shield out of it. The way she kept anyone else who wanted to get close to her at a safe distance. She knew it was crazy, and she wouldn't admit it to anyone else, but part of her understood Olivia's views on love.

"I think you're right. I think the worst thing we can do is trust people just because we want to believe they love us. That's what I did with Phinn."

Olivia nodded. "I may be a lot older than you, but we're not that different."

"I guess not."

Olivia unhooked Wylie from the heart monitor and said there was something she wanted to show her in the employee wing of BioLark. The staff had taken to referring to that portion of the building as the "forbidden side." It was off limits to the kids and only accessible with an ID tag. Wylie had seen parts of the wing on the day they'd arrived in BioLark, but she hadn't been back since. The blinding fluorescent lights and the *tap-tap* of Olivia's heels hitting the ground in a frenetic rhythm raised her anxiety despite the *rahat* in her system. She had no idea where they were going.

The hallways were endless. They turned left and then right and then left again. She lost track of how they'd gotten here and wasn't sure she'd be able to find her way back to the other side of the lab on her own. Then Olivia hit a button on the wall and two giant doors swung open. She guided Wylie through the entrance and quickened her pace, making the *tap-tap* sounds grow closer together. There was an excitement to her gait that reminded Wylie of the day Phinn had first brought her to the island. Maybe they were going to Olivia's office so Wylie could test out her sofa cushions and they could dig into pints of ice cream and talk more about boys.

"We're here," Olivia announced, as she opened a door to a hospital room.

Dr. Jay was real. He was not a figment of Wylie's imagination. And he was lying in a hospital bed with his eyes closed.

"What happened to him?" Wylie asked.

"He betrayed me. Just like Phinn. Just like everyone does," Olivia said. "I know why he brought you here, Wylie. He was asking too many questions and gave himself away."

"You're wrong," Wylie lied. "We were the ones he was tricking."

Olivia stifled a laugh. "It's sweet to watch you defend him, but I don't buy it. You're the same girl who ignored me for weeks, and just tried to bond with me over Phinn. You might as well wear a T-shirt that says 'I have ulterior motives.'"

Plastic tubes poked out of Dr. Jay's nose and his chest slowly moved up and down. If it wasn't for that, he would have appeared peaceful and content. But instead, he looked like he was a prisoner in his own body.

I tried to help you, Wylie could picture him saying. *I'm so sorry.*

Hot tears raced down her face. Wylie tried to get rid of them, but it felt like a pipe had burst in her tear duct. The combination of relief and terror were difficult to reconcile—relief that her intuition had been right about Dr. Jay, terror over what had happened to him.

"What did you do to him?" Wylie managed to ask.

"He's in a medically induced coma," Olivia replied calmly.

The tears came even faster, but Wylie used them to her advantage. She flung her body over Dr. Jay's hospital bed, and sobbed dramatically, hoping to distract Olivia in the process. She glimpsed Dr. Jay's forearms, but they were scrubbed clean. There were no traces of the ink he'd used to scribble down notes on the island. Wylie remembered that he was left handed, so she grabbed his right hand and grazed her finger on the palm.

"It's not right what you're doing!" she screamed at Olivia. "He's a good person. You didn't have to hurt him!"

"I had no choice," Olivia said, coldly. "Accept your fate, Wylie. You're not getting out of here. But you don't have to worry about Lola or her baby. I'll take good care of them."

Wylie wouldn't allow herself to be distracted by threats. She quickly separated Dr. Jay's fingers, making it seem like she wanted to interlace them with her own, and that's when she spotted the words scribbled between his index and middle fingers. The ink was smudged and faded, but Wylie could still string together the phrase:

Quiet at the punchbowl

She used the clamminess of her palm to smudge up the ink further, so that Olivia would never see it.

Wylie wiped away her tears and followed Olivia out of the room. This time, they took a shorter route out of the staff quarters that led them straight to the deck where the dining room was located.

Quiet at the punchbowl. Wylie wasn't sure what it meant, but she assumed Dr. Jay was deliberately vague with his note. He didn't want Olivia or anyone else at BioLark to know that he was trying to give their lab rats a clue.

A punchbowl conjured up images of a high school dance. It was the place for teenagers to mill around awkwardly, while watching everyone else enjoy themselves. What did it mean in the context of BioLark? Wylie assumed it was a clue that he'd recently discovered or one he'd kept to himself for insurance purposes.

Olivia escorted her to the dining room in time for dinner. They usually served sandwiches on stale bread accompanied by an overripe banana or canned pineapple. She took her regular seat across from Hopper and hoped he wouldn't be able to tell that she'd been crying. Wylie worried he'd resort to violence if he learned about Dr. Jay's coma.

She wished it was safe to pick Hopper's brain about the message on his finger. Maybe it referenced something from their shared past in foster care, or maybe it was just something totally arbitrary he'd scribbled down out of boredom. *Quiet at the Punchbowl* could be the title of a book or the name of a new band that Wylie had never heard of. It could mean anything.

"You seem pensive," Hopper said.

"I'm just tired," Wylie lied.

"Let's go to the fake Clearing," Hopper suggested. "We can hang out together before everyone else piles in and we're tailed by nurses and orderlies all night. Let's have some fun for a change."

They weren't technically allowed to leave the dining hall until everyone was finished with their meals, but Wylie didn't care. This place couldn't get much worse, and she wasn't going to live in fear of getting disciplined by the likes of Olivia or Nurse Conway. There was no harm in taking a private flight with Hopper before everyone else bombarded them.

"Okay, let's go."

Wylie caught Phinn staring at them as they made their way out of the room, and took mild pleasure in the look of longing and jealousy on his face. *Good*, Wylie thought. It was only fair that he felt some of the hurt, too.

"I feel like swimming," Hopper announced when they reached the lagoon.

A few orderlies stood at their usual posts, but none of them seemed alarmed by their presence. Maybe they wanted to give them an opportunity to have a little fun, too.

"In that?" Wylie asked, pointing to the concrete tub they were supposed to pretend was a lagoon. The high chlorine content made it smell like a public swimming pool that had seen a lot of action.

"We can close our eyes and pretend we're on the island," he said.

"Not even Dr. Seuss had that good of an imagination," Wylie joked.

But it felt good to go for a dip in the water, even if it was laced with chemicals to keep it clean. The cold liquid loosened Wylie's sore muscles, and when she floated on her back, the palm trees obscured the mounted fans and cameras that made it obvious they were confined to an indoor space. Hopper floated past her on his back, and their arms touched as they drifted next to each other. It was peaceful here. It was always peaceful with Hopper.

"I feel like an awful person," Hopper confessed.

"Why?"

"I've been sharing a bungalow with Bandit. I didn't know he was so far gone. I had no idea he was going to try to kill himself."

Bandit's eighteenth birthday had taken them by surprise. He hadn't told anyone his days were numbered until it was too late. Wylie had observed his behavior before the night he'd jumped off the deck, and though he seemed more reserved than usual, she never would have guessed he was suicidal.

"Everyone's depressed," she told Hopper. "It's impossible to know which one of us has hit rock bottom when we're all so close to it."

"Yeah, but I'm *living* with the guy."

Wylie placed her hands on Hopper's face and made sure

he was looking right at her. She wanted him to pay attention.

"You can't rescue everyone, Hopper," she said.

The waterfall crashed down behind them. Wylie knew a switch operated it, because she never heard it at night when they went to sleep. The conversation was getting too heavy, and Wylie wanted to give Hopper a laugh. She pushed him into the waterfall and dunked him beneath it. He managed to grab her legs and pull her down with him. She opened her eyes under water and saw him wading in front of her with a smile on his face. She wished they could break through the surface and magically find themselves back in the real lagoon and in the real Clearing. Hopper went up for air first and Wylie followed. None of the orderlies could see them behind the waterfall, but it was only a matter of minutes before they stepped into the lagoon to make sure they weren't doing anything illicit. Just the other night, they'd dragged a partially dressed Micah and Tinka out from behind it.

"What?" Wylie asked, as Hopper stared at her.

"Nothing," he replied.

He was going to kiss her. Wylie could feel it. She wanted to let him. She wanted to feel like a normal teenager for five minutes. She wanted one thing to be happy about, even if it complicated their friendship or ruined it completely. The end was always painful, after all.

Quiet at the punchbowl.

The words suddenly had new meaning as Hopper moved his face toward hers. She abruptly pulled back, startled by her own revelation.

A punchbowl was a type of waterfall. Wylie knew this

because a couple years ago, her mom and dad had gotten into an argument over the locale of their next family vacation. Wylie's mom wanted to fly to Paris and Wylie's dad wanted to go to Punch Bowl Falls in Oregon. None of them had even heard of Punch Bowl Falls. Wylie had Googled it and read that it was responsible for the waterfall classification of a "punchbowl," which described a current that descends in a constricted form and spreads out into a wider pool. Now Wylie realized why her father wanted so badly to visit it. Punch Bowl Falls reminded him of the lagoon and the island. But Maura had won the argument and they'd gone to Paris instead.

Dr. Jay was trying to tell them there was one area in BioLark where they could speak without being recorded or eavesdropped on. It's quiet at the punchbowl.

"We can say anything we want *here*," Wylie exclaimed. "We can come up with a plan. Lola's not going to have her baby here. We're going to find a way out."

"Wylie, stop. They're listening, remember? They're always listening."

"Not here, they're not," Wylie said.

The waterfall was their safe harbor. And Wylie planned to use it to set them free.

old habits die hard

phinn tried to examine his shoulder blades in the mirror, but glimpsing the reflection of his torn-up flesh made him dizzy and lightheaded. His body was starting to build up a high tolerance to *rahat* pills, and the constant throbbing from the cuts and burns Nurse Conway had inflicted on his back was increasing in intensity. The experiments were allegedly supposed to test out the effectiveness of the medication, but Phinn wondered if they were actually just an elaborate excuse to torture him. He blinked a few times to focus his vision and study the state of his wounds. Some were healing, but others bubbled over with pus and blood. Once the scars settled in, his skin would look like an abstract painting. He was glad the BioLark staff had used his back as their canvas instead of his chest or his face. Right now, he wished that Olivia had also harvested *dava* plants, so that their cooling agents would help quiet the burning sensation.

"It's infected," Tinka said, as she entered the bungalow and interrupted his private pity party.

Her straw-colored hair was wet from what was probably another make out session with Micah near the waterfall. The pixie cut she usually sported had grown out to frame her face with ringlets that were currently drizzling water on their bungalow floor. In all the years they'd known each other, Phinn had never realized she had curly hair. The signature scowl that he'd always thought was just the natural state of her face was now replaced with a permanent smile. He was glad to witness this new version of Tinka. She gave him hope that in time a person could change.

"Can you help me put the ointment on?" Phinn asked.

"I guess," Tinka mumbled.

Nurse Conway had left them a tube of antibiotic cream and told them to use it regularly to avoid infection. Phinn had been ignoring his advice because he'd been desperate to feel the pain. He'd been desperate to feel *anything*. The steady cocktail of meds made him sleepwalk through the days. As long as they were in a fog, they'd never be able to figure out an exit strategy.

"Ouch," he blurted. The light touch of Tinka's fingertips made his pain sing like a death growl.

"Sorry," Tinka replied. "I'll try to be gentle."

He wasn't sure why, out of everyone, Tinka was still nice to him. Maybe it was out of habit. Phinn had done wrong by her over and over again, and she'd always forgiven him. Maybe she just didn't know how to stay mad at him. Their history book had its fair share of conflict, but there were also passages of reprieve. After their parents had died, he slept on the floor of Tinka's bungalow for years because she was too afraid to sleep alone. It was strange now to remember a time when Tinka was afraid of anything.

"You're the only one who doesn't ignore me around these parts," Phinn pointed out.

"We're sharing a bungalow. It's kind of hard to ignore you."

"But you volunteered to sleep here. You didn't have to do that."

Phinn felt a cool breeze against his wounds. Tinka was gently blowing on them.

"I don't hate you," she said. "What you did to Lola was a new low. It was more than I thought you were ever capable of. I can't even be ten feet away from Hopper without wanting to bury myself alive after what we put him through. But Micah's the best thing that ever happened to me. If you weren't so demented and crazy, he wouldn't exist. And he would have never come to the island. So I'm grateful to you for that."

Phinn nodded. He remembered sitting next to Micah on the rooftop in Brooklyn, as he sulked into his flask and stared at his phone. They'd exchanged a few words, but Micah hadn't seemed interested in making a new friend. In the brief time they spent together, Phinn was struck by how much the boy reminded him of Tinka. He was he glad he'd recruited someone who loved her the way she deserved to be loved. Someone who could be everything to her that he couldn't. And yet, it hurt to see her so happy. Phinn had no one left who loved him like that.

"How'd you get out of skipping the evening's festivities?" Tinka asked.

"I told Olivia I wasn't feeling well," Phinn admitted.

He knew it was a lame excuse considering *none* of them felt well, but he needed one night to hide in his bungalow. His heart might collapse from watching Maz and Lola laugh and coo as they felt their baby kick. The other night, he'd heard them giggling over fake baby name suggestions like Woodmeg or Chipney. During happier times with Wylie, he'd imagined what it might be like to have children together, how they'd be much better parents than the ones Phinn had.

"Well, you didn't miss much," Tinka said. "I think Olivia actually thinks we like her. She got up on stage again to sing with Bailey. Ugh. She's such an elder."

It was surprising how little Olivia had changed since her teen years. She used to love singing to Phinn when she lived on the island.

"I almost forgot," Tinka lowered her voice to a barely audible whisper. "Wylie wants you to meet her in the waterfall tomorrow night."

The pain must have been playing tricks on his hearing.

"Is this some elaborate prank?" Phinn asked. "Are you guys looking for more ways to make a fool of me?"

"Nope."

Wylie and Phinn hadn't spoken since her arrival, but Phinn figured she had a few festering emotions to purge. Maybe Olivia had prescribed her primal therapy, and Phinn was the person she wanted to direct her vitriol at. He slowly put his shirt on and let the ointment seep into the abrasions. Tonight he would have to sleep on his stomach, but hopefully, by morning, the aching would subside. He was wrong to think he wanted to feel it. To be numb was a far better way to function.

* * * * * * *

THE FOLLOWING DAY MOVED AT AN EXCRUCIATING pace. Phinn had mentally prepared himself for every terrible insult Wylie would sling his way. He wasn't surprised to be the first one to show up at their meeting spot. The water was lukewarm, but at least it cleared away the sweat gathering at his brow. The lagoon shifted around him as Wylie approached. He turned to face her.

All his preparation was useless. There were dark circles under Wylie's eyes and her hair looked like she hadn't brushed it in days. Her lips were cracked and dry, and a trail of acne was scattered across her forehead. She was the most beautiful thing he'd ever seen.

"Thanks for meeting me here," she said.

"Thanks for asking."

He took a step toward her, but she was quick to move away from him

"I have a plan to get us out of here," Wylie confessed.

He placed his index finger to his lips to signal to Wylie to stop talking. After their failed prison break, he knew there were probably bugs installed across every inch of the place.

"It's okay," Wylie said. "They can't hear us here. I have a plan, but I can't do it without you."

"What do you want me to do?" he asked.

"Seduce Olivia," Wylie responded, flatly. "She's desperate for your approval and we need her distracted for as long as possible."

Wylie was calm. She seemed utterly indifferent to Phinn. He felt *everything* when he was around her: the entire gamut of human emotions, backward and forward. And it was clear she felt less than nothing.

"You want me to seduce Olivia?" he echoed.

"It's what you're good at, isn't it?"

Phinn cocked his head and struggled to stop himself from smiling. Wylie wasn't indifferent at all. How could she be when she clearly resented the hell out of him?

"So I've been told," Phinn replied. "When do you suggest I do this?"

"Tomorrow night at your therapy session. Keep her away from her office and the Clearing for as long as you can."

Phinn finally had a chance to redeem himself. He would dole out the right compliments and chuckle when Olivia said anything remotely funny. He would fool a woman who hated him into thinking he was worthy of her affection. But he didn't want to agree to the plan right away and cut his meeting with Wylie short.

"I don't think Olivia will—"

"*Get your hands off me!*"

The voice that cut him off was muffled through the

crashing sounds of the waterfall, but it was clearly Lola's, loud and frantic enough to send them hurrying back to the Clearing. Lola was kicking and flailing as two orderlies picked her up and laid her down on a stretcher. They strapped her arms and legs to the gurney as she continued to beg them to let her go.

"Calm down!" Olivia demanded. "Stress is bad for the baby."

"What are you doing to her?" Wylie yelled.

"Not that it's any of your business, but her last set of blood work showed an abnormality. We have to run more tests. If she stops putting up a fight, we won't have to keep her strapped to the bed," Olivia explained.

"She's scared to be alone with you," Wylie argued. "Let me come with her."

Phinn let out a heavy sigh, shook his head, and turned to Olivia.

"The woman's trying to do her job, Wylie," he said. "For the love of God, why don't you stop inserting yourself into other people's lives."

Olivia gave him a confused look, but didn't bother to question his motives.

"Thank you, Phinn," she said. "But I'd never deprive someone of moral support. Maz, you can come with us."

Lola quieted down once Maz placed his hand on her forehead, and stayed in step with the orderlies and Olivia as they carted her away. Phinn kept his eyes fixed on them, certain that Olivia wouldn't be able to help herself and not look back.

5 . . . 4 . . . 3 . . . 2 . . . 1 . . .

Olivia glanced over her shoulder and Phinn gave her his best alluring grin. He swore he caught her smiling before she turned back around.

Wylie was right. This *was* what he was good at.

trust issues

"YOU seem perky this evening," Olivia observed.

"I've turned over a new leaf."

"Interesting," Olivia said, as she scribbled down something on her notepad. "What brought about the change?"

Phinn shrugged casually. "I guess I finally accepted that I'm never going back to the island. Even if you decided your research was complete and that we were a burden to you here, I would have to live in exile. They hate me."

"With good reason," Olivia was quick to add.

"Yes. With good reason. But living here is the best alternative. It looks *exactly* like home."

Phinn noticed an instant shift in Olivia's posture. She straightened her shoulders and lifted her chin. He could only imagine the amount of money and resources she'd poured into building her own version of Minor Island.

"I tried so hard make it look authentic. I would have preferred to study you in your natural habitat, but I knew that wasn't possible. The last thing I needed was to get the life choked out of me by *parvaz* vines."

Phinn made sure to hang on her every word, while Olivia listed off her grand plans for BioLark. She'd recently enlisted the same landscaper who'd designed the Clearing to help create their own *parvaz* field. She wished it could be as vast as the one on the island, but at least it would be big enough for picnics and midnight strolls.

"We're going to plant our own willow tree," she said, excitedly.

The flowers they'd genetically modified didn't make the same *pop-pop* sounds they were famous for back home, but Olivia was going to install hidden speakers beneath the vines to replicate the tone.

"That's so awesome," Phinn proclaimed.

He leaned in and scratched the scar in his eyebrow. Olivia looked away for a fleeting moment until she changed her mind and held his gaze.

"Did Wylie tell you about the night she flew away from the island?" Phinn asked.

"She doesn't tell me much of anything."

"She fell into the ocean," Phinn confessed. "She was so eager to get away from me that she was willing to risk her life to do it."

Phinn went on, hoping Olivia would take his bait.

"I hit rock bottom when I lost Wylie, but I pulled myself up. I hate having to see her every day. It's just a reminder that she brought out the worst in me. Not like *you*. You brought out the best in me when we were together."

Phinn placed his hand on top of her palm, and Olivia let him.

"They say the hands are a dead giveaway when it comes to someone's age," Olivia said, looking at hers self-consciously. "You can get a hundred rounds of Botox, but people can always tell how old you are when they look at your hands. Mine are so wrinkled now."

"I think they look porcelain," said Phinn, trying to sound sincere.

The truth was, her hands were soft and warm to the touch. There was something maternal in the way she moved that actually made him crave being in her presence. His interactions with adults during his trips to the mainland had been few and far between. He usually preferred to ask fellow teenagers for directions on the subway or whether they knew about any parties he could crash in search of new recruits. The only time he spoke to grown-ups was if he got hungry and needed to stop somewhere for fast food.

"Do you want to go for a flight together?" Phinn asked Olivia.

"No," she answered flatly.

"I don't mean *here*," he said. "I mean outside."

"That's not possible."

"Why? Because people could see us?"

Olivia shook her head. "There isn't anyone other than BioLark staff around for miles."

"Then why not?"

"Because I don't trust you," she replied.

"I just want to see the real sky," he begged. "With you. Like the night we met."

"It was so long ago, I can barely remember," she said dismissively, but Phinn knew she was lying. He was certain she played the highlight reel in her head more times than she'd care to admit. If she were truly over him, then she would have moved on with her life. She'd have kids to go home to and maybe a husband who'd surprise her with flowers when there was no occasion for them. The island and Phinn and everyone else would be a distant memory.

"Remember when your grandma saw us flying?" Phinn asked.

"No. I told you. I don't remember much about that night," replied Olivia, but her smile betrayed her.

Even Phinn couldn't help but laugh at the memory. Olivia's wealthy and uptight grandmother had been drinking a dirty martini on the balcony of the mansion when she saw Phinn and Olivia fly by and flash her their middle fingers. She promptly spilled the drink on herself and started ranting and raving that she'd seen the ghost of her granddaughter. Everyone assumed it was the first signs of dementia, but Phinn knew the tirade would give them chills when they found Olivia's bedroom empty the next morning.

"Do you know what happened to her?" Phinn asked.

"She died," Olivia said. "Just weeks after you sent me into exile. Your timing wasn't bad. At least it gave her an opportunity to put me back in her will."

"See," Phinn said. "There's always a silver lining."

He tickled the palm of her hand and insisted that the best way to honor her grandmother's memory was for them to take flight together.

"You're the expert on *parvaz*," Phinn argued. "You know

the exact dosage that would prevent me from flying away."

It took a little more cajoling, but Olivia finally relented. She warned him that the small dose of *parvaz* she was giving him would last a mere fifteen minutes, and she was also going to keep a Taser in her pocket and a syringe full of sedatives in case he had any ideas about getting away.

"Honestly, Olivia. Where would I go? I've got food in my belly and a bed to sleep in and you're not even charging me rent."

They walked along the deck, past the Clearing and the kids trickling in from dinner. Phinn expected them to make their way through the lab, but Olivia escorted him into a bungalow instead.

Had his skills of seduction worked *too* well? Was she going to expect him to sleep with her? She turned on a light in the bungalow, and Phinn breathed a sigh of relief to see there was no bed in it. Aside from a chair, the room was completely bare. Olivia dragged the chair to the center of the floor and Phinn watched as she stood on top of it. She used her BioLark card to scan the ceiling and a door slid open. A ladder made out of rope came swinging down.

Olivia climbed the ladder first and waited for Phinn to follow. He was surprised to feel the warmth of the sun against his skin. It was nighttime inside BioLark, but daytime in real life. She took Phinn's hand and helped pull him up to the rooftop of the dome-shaped building. She was right. There was nobody here for miles. They were in the thick of the forest.

"It's nothing like the island out here," she said, somewhat sheepishly.

"I know," Phinn agreed, "But that's why I like it."

Phinn hardly noticed that they were still holding hands as they levitated to the treetops. He could have escaped if he'd wanted. He could have squirmed out of her grip and flown away before she had a chance to use her Taser or inject him with liquid sleep.

But he decided against it. He wasn't going to abandon Wylie and the others.

* * * * * * *

THE FINER POINTS OF WYLIE'S PLAN HAD ONLY BEEN discussed a few times. It was nothing like those weeks on Hopper's boat when they'd dissected each bullet point of Operation Exile in painful detail. Their bevy of chaperones and rigid schedules didn't afford them the luxury of fleshing out every scenario or coming up with fail-safe excuses if they got caught. Pulling it off would require strong instincts, the ability to improvise, and complete fearlessness. They were all traits that Wylie felt she no longer possessed. It was easy to second-guess herself without any tips or assurances from her best friend, but there had been no sign of Lola and Maz since Olivia had wheeled her out of the Clearing the night before.

Before she met Phinn, Wylie used to be confident about her choices—however impulsive or risky they were. She was never indecisive. Her old best friend Vanessa used to have lengthy internal debates about every mundane event in her life. If she wanted a new haircut, it meant months of compiling styles to her Pinterest board and agonizing over which look would best flatter her face. Meanwhile, Wylie was the type who woke up craving a change, and walked right into a salon with a precise idea of what she wanted. The voice of self-doubt that questioned her every thought and action was a recent addition. For today, Wylie would have to ignore it.

Tinka was tasked with keeping tabs on Phinn and Olivia. But as Tinka glided toward the lagoon, Wylie couldn't tell whether she had good or bad news to report. She landed on her feet, took a minor stumble, and waited until none of the orderlies were paying attention to her. She cleared her throat and gave a subtle nod toward the deck, then walked away toward Hopper and Micah. Wylie glanced at the deck and spotted Phinn trailing behind Dr. Weckler. She wondered how much charisma and fake vulnerability he had to exude to get on her good side again. After years of harbored angst, how had Phinn convinced her to give him the benefit of the doubt with one brief conversation? Wylie would never be fooled so easily by a guy again. She'd happily be alone forever rather than have the rug pulled out from under her by someone she loved.

They disappeared into a bungalow and closed the door.

Wylie grabbed the elastic on her wrist and tied her hair into a messy ponytail. The action triggered her least favorite stage of their plan. It wouldn't be fun watching her youngest brother get his ass handed to him, but they needed to create a diversion.

"Tell your girlfriend to get away from me," Hopper snapped at Micah.

"Tell her yourself. I'm not your mouthpiece," Micah replied.

If Wylie could yell "cut," she would have interrupted to tell Micah to take his anger up a few notches.

"I don't want the crazy bitch anywhere near me." Hopper's acting abilities were far more convincing, but he had plenty of motivation. Tinka wasn't exactly his favorite person.

"Don't you ever call her that again," Micah yelled. Tinka pulled at his arm and insisted that she could fight her own battles, but Hopper wouldn't stop.

"She cut off my fingers," Hopper yelled back. "I think that makes me entitled to call her a crazy bitch."

Hopper put his hands on Micah's chest and shoved him so hard he fell to the ground. Micah scrambled to his feet and reciprocated the push. Wylie hurried over and tried to get between them, but Hopper grabbed her brother in a headlock and wrestled him into the dirt. The orderlies and nurses were quick to surround them, but none volunteered to step in. Without Olivia, they were afraid of the kids. Their last act of rebellion had left Nurse Conway permanently blind in one eye.

But a quick escalation of one-way punches from Hopper made it seem like Wylie's only recourse was to shout for help.

"Do something! They're going to kill each other!" she begged the staff.

Nurse Conway finally intervened and pulled Hopper off Micah. Hopper kicked and shrieked as Nurse Conway dragged him away. He was brave, Wylie thought. The punishment for fighting was a night spent beneath the floorboards of the dining hall. Bandit had suffered the same consequence for trying to take his own life, and said the room was pitch black and freezing cold. She knew it would be traumatic for Hopper to spend an entire night in close quarters by himself.

She watched as Hopper writhed and yelled at Nurse Conway to back off. His vehemence was so realistic that if Wylie hadn't known he was faking it, she'd be afraid of him. Hopper was unhinged and intense in all the ways they needed him to be for their plan to succeed. It was no wonder the other kids had spent so much time convinced he was going to kill them. He seemed capable of anything. Wylie carefully made her approach and pretended to try to get Hopper to calm down.

"You need to breathe. Stop acting crazy. Tell Nurse Conway you're sorry," she kept repeating.

"*Screw that!*" Hopper yelled, sending several drops of spit onto her cheek.

Wylie grabbed his arm, obscured him with her body, and firmly told him to calm down. But Hopper's legs flew in the air and forced her to back away. She hoped the rest of the employees hadn't notice the sleight of hand. Just as it looked like he might kick her, Hopper had placed Nurse Conway's ID tag in the pocket of Wylie's scrubs.

As Nurse Conway dragged Hopper away toward solitary, Wylie was suddenly startled by a sensation that she might never see him again. The minutiae of their plan had taken up so much of her focus that she'd never stopped to think what could happen if it fell apart. She wished that they'd said a proper good-bye when they had the chance. If she had less on her mind, she would have let him kiss her under the downpour of the waterfall.

"Are you okay?" she asked Micah, while he fought to catch his breath.

The abrasions and soon-to-be bruises on his face would take weeks to properly heal. Wylie and Joshua pretended to scold and lecture him for his anger issues, and Micah reacted by cursing Hopper under his breath. The BioLark staff had already retreated to their usual posts along the Clearing, so Wylie approached a nearby orderly who was known to be more pleasant than his colleagues. She smiled at him sweetly, apologized for the chaos, and asked for permission to retire to their bungalow so Micah could simmer down. The orderly insisted on escorting them back to their bungalow, but en route to their room, they heard Nurse Conway yelling for help with Hopper. As luck would have it, the orderly hurried off and Wylie and her brothers slipped away in the opposite direction.

The three of them rushed past the bungalows, through the dining room, and toward the wing of the BioLark labs that led to Olivia's office. Wylie hadn't seen her office since the day they'd been herded into the building, but hoped they would be able to navigate the maze of hallways until they found it. A pair of wide metal doors blocked their way through the entrance, but Wylie waved Nurse Conway's ID card in front of them, and they swung open.

There was plenty Wylie liked about wearing scrubs every day. Not only were they airy and comfortable, but they also didn't do much to differentiate them from the BioLark staff. If they moved quickly enough, anyone who caught a glimpse of them on a security monitor would think they were nurses on their way to a meeting.

But the corridors intersected more times than Wylie remembered, and every left or right turn felt like it could be taking them further away from Olivia's office. She knew Dr. Jay's hospital room was near the dining room, but she had no clue where it was in association to Olivia's office. Hopefully Phinn was whispering enough sweet nothings to keep Olivia distracted.

"Do you know where we're going?" Joshua asked.

"I think so," Wylie lied.

If only she still had the compass that Joshua gave her, so that she could keep track of each turn they'd taken. They reached another crossroad of hallways and glanced down each one. The smell of coconut and pineapple suddenly hit Wylie's nostrils.

"This way," she said, pointing toward the direction the fruity notes were wafting from. Before they could follow the scent, they spotted an orderly walking toward them and glancing at his phone.

They turned around and pressed their bodies against the wall, silently praying that he would turn down a different corner. Instead, he walked right past them, never peeling his eyes away from his device. After months without an iPhone, Wylie had forgotten how hypnotic they could be.

Once the orderly was a safe distance away, they turned and headed toward what was hopefully Olivia's office. They finally reached the end of the hallway and found a lone door next to an elevator bank. The fragrance of tropical fruit was so strong that it made Wylie's eyes water. She reached for the knob and let out a surprised gasp when she realized the door wasn't locked.

The lights were off when they tiptoed into the office, but turned on automatically once they sensed movement. Wylie quietly closed the door behind them. She checked the clock on the wall. The time read noon, which was odd considering it was bedtime beyond the labs and offices.

"I'm giving us five minutes," she said. "Keep your eye on the time."

Wylie felt like they were playing the bonus round on a game show, as the second hand ticked and they swiftly rifled through drawers and files, looking for maps or blueprints of tunnels that could help get them home. The first phase of their plan was finding the exit, and then they might have to wait days to enact an exit strategy.

The drawers were meticulously organized and color-coded. Olivia kept files with notes from each of their therapy sessions, along with results from the daily tests and experiments they were forced to undergo. Wylie's eyes went wide when she found several ultrasound photos in Lola's file. She decided to pocket them so they could be returned to their rightful owners. She felt a twinge of guilt as she glimpsed Joshua's files and saw enough to know his therapy sessions were devoted to Katie Anderson and his guilt about the accident in the Hamptons that had put her in a coma.

The clock read 12:03 p.m. Their window was closing. Wylie had no idea how long Phinn would be able to keep Olivia or what could happen if they got caught. They might be put in medically induced comas, just like Dr. Jay. If they didn't find information on the supposed tunnels, they might never make it beyond the walls of BioLark. Lola would have her baby here. They would all turn eighteen and then none of them would be able to return to the island anyway.

She looked at the phone and computer sitting on Olivia's desk.

"Screw the island," Wylie said aloud.

Micah and Joshua turned to look at her as she grabbed the telephone on the desk. She tried to dial 9-1-1 but the line was dead.

"What are you doing?" Micah asked.

"Getting us out of here."

Wylie sat down at Olivia's computer, but the screen was locked and required a password. She typed in MINOR ISLAND, but that was invalid. PHINN and BIOLARK also didn't work.

"You're never going to guess her password," Joshua said.

But there was one more she wanted to try. Wylie quickly typed in the words: BEYOND COMPARE and found herself logged in to Olivia's desktop. She double-clicked on the web browser and quickly navigated it to the Facebook homepage. It had been a while since she'd accessed her account, but her password, Microplane1, for her favorite cooking accessory, still worked. She ignored the hundreds of notifications and went straight to the Facebook Live option.

Wylie looked straight into the camera and spoke as quickly as possible:

"My name is Wylie Dalton. I went missing from New York City with my brothers several months ago. A woman named Olivia Weckler is keeping us in a facility in upstate New York. I don't know where we are exactly. It was about a three-hour drive from Manhattan. The roads were covered in potholes. We turned left at the train tracks. We walked a mile through the woods across three streams. It smelled like maple or fenugreek. We are in danger. There are fifty other kids—"

The door burst open and a furious Olivia stood in the frame. A worried Phinn stood beside her. Wylie quickly closed the window on the computer.

"What the hell are you doing in my office?" Olivia yelled.

Phinn moved in front of Olivia and used his arm to block her way.

"Don't punish them," he said. "This was my idea. They didn't do anything wrong. I promise."

Olivia pushed her way past Phinn and grabbed Wylie by her hair.

"Do you think I'm an idiot?" Olivia asked.

"Yes," Wylie snapped back. "You fell for it. You thought Phinn wanted to spend alone time with you. He played you again."

"Then I guess he'll need to be punished," Olivia said coldly.

Wylie felt something pinch her skin. She didn't know what was happening to her, but from the sober expressions on her brothers' faces, she knew everything was about to get worse. It didn't matter. Olivia was too late. Someone would see her video. Someone would try to find them.

"He told me I was beyond compare, too, Olivia. He says it to all the girls."

The back of Olivia's hand came rushing toward Wylie's face, but she didn't care. She knew she wouldn't feel a thing.

moving on

"*YOU deserve each other.*"

Those were Olivia's parting words. Her outburst was dramatically punctuated by a door slam, the *clink* of a bolt lock, and the *tap-tap* of her high heels drifting away. Phinn looked at Wylie, sedated in the corner, and wasn't sure if he should try to wake her or let her rest. Phinn knew the moment she woke up and learned they were locked in a padded cell together, she'd claw at the walls and scream for help until her throat was as rough as coral.

He'd let her down again. He was supposed to keep Olivia occupied and it had started out fine. They'd traveled the perimeter of the building for a few minutes, reminiscing about "the Minor Island glory days," as Olivia called them. After laughing at a few memories, she wanted his version of the falling out with Gregory.

"I only know his side of the story," she said.

Phinn gave a dramatic monologue that crescendoed

with a mea culpa. He'd been selfish and immature. He hated being the third wheel and couldn't shake the feeling that Tinka and Gregory didn't want him around anymore. His jealousy fooled him into thinking he was in love with Tinka, and he pledged his devotion to lure her back.

"I took her away from my best friend," Phinn confessed, "And I didn't even really want to be with her. It was an elder move."

"You always were a piece of work," Olivia said.

Phinn tried to find a natural segue to BioLark and Olivia's research. He asked if they were making any progress. After weeks of submitting to blood tests and biopsies for tissue samples, he hoped the answer was yes. The thought had occurred to him that if she could actually figure out a way to keep mankind from aging, Phinn could stay young without returning to the island.

"We're making baby steps," admitted Olivia. "It's a slow process. We might need to take a future trip to the island, but that would require your full cooperation."

With two of her staff already dead from their excursion on the island, none of Olivia's surviving employees were willing to follow in their footsteps. Olivia didn't have much desire to put herself at risk either. But they could return and seek refuge on a boat while Phinn and a select few gathered materials for them.

"Think of yourself as a liaison between me and the island," Olivia said. "We'd conduct the studies on my boat, and it would be your job to bring us what we needed."

Phinn acted like it would be an honor to pitch in, but he

wanted to laugh at the absurdity of the offer. Agreeing to help Olivia Weckler would be like giving his soul to the devil for free.

"Or this will be a moot point and we'll get everything we need from Lola's baby," Olivia added, "Those are going to be some very valuable stem cells."

"Where is Lola exactly?" Phinn asked.

"On bed rest."

He wanted to tell Olivia to keep her hands off Maz and Lola's baby. But any defiance would blow his cover and send them back into the building.

"Do you want to take a break?" he asked instead.

Phinn was already flying more slowly than normal, but Olivia still had trouble keeping up. Her breathing was labored as she struggled to fly and talk at the same time. The dark liner around her eyes was smudged and her unruly curls were damp from perspiration. She was either terribly out of shape or displaying the normal side effects of middle age.

The dose of *parvaz* would be running out soon anyway. They sat on the rooftop together, and Phinn made it seem like he was equally burned out from the flight. Once her breathing returned to normal, Olivia resumed their conversation.

"I need to thank you for something," she said.

"What?"

"For exiling me. I thought it was cruel what you did, but you probably saved my life. I was eighteen and the island wouldn't have allowed me to survive anyway. I thought

I was just accident-prone at the time, but the place was already trying to get rid of me."

"What do you mean?" Phinn asked.

Olivia described a few falls and mishaps that could have been a coincidence or a direct result of being an adult on the island. They would never know for sure, but Phinn decided to pounce on the latter scenario.

Phinn smiled. "See?" he teased. "I always had your best interests at heart."

"Did you miss me at all?" she asked.

The honest answer would have been no. It didn't take Phinn long to get over Olivia. He'd been looking for an excuse to break up with her before her gray hairs appeared. By the time Maz got back from leaving her in New York, Phinn had already moved on to someone else. He couldn't even remember who it had been.

"Every day," Phinn said.

Olivia tilted her face toward his. He wasn't sure if she was going to kiss him or if she just wanted to decipher whether he was telling the truth. Either way, the sudden proximity made him flinch and he leaned away instinctively.

"We should go back inside," Olivia said crisply.

Phinn asked if they could enjoy the fresh air for a few more minutes, but Olivia insisted that they'd been gone for too long.

"It's almost past your bedtime," she said.

Phinn looked up at the sun-streaked sky and decided not to point out that it was actually daytime. They made their way down the ladder and into the bungalow again, and before they stepped out the door, Olivia asked if he was interested in a nightcap in her office.

"I've got a couple of sugar roots with your name on them," she cooed.

He tried to come up with excuses for them to join the party in the Clearing instead. Like how the other kids would only have more reason to hate him if they thought he was receiving special treatment. Or that he was feeling tired and disoriented from the daylight. She should save the sugar roots for herself. But Olivia refused to take no for an answer.

"I'm the leader here, Phinn," she reminded him.

It wasn't until they moved past the double doors in the dining room that Phinn realized that she wasn't luring him into her office to seduce him. Olivia suspected something was off. Her legs moved quickly through the sterile hallway, and Phinn had to speed walk just to keep up.

"I wasn't going to kiss you, Phinn," she said, her voice shaky. "I'm old enough to be your mother."

Please, Phinn prayed. *Please let Wylie not be in her office anymore*. But apparently no gods were listening.

Now the sound of Wylie's snores broke up the other ambient noises, and Phinn stole glances at her as she slept. She looked so different from the night she'd passed out on his boat, completely unaware that they were sailing to a magical island. Right now, Wylie was only a couple of months older than when they met, but the lines across her forehead made her look like she'd spent a few dismal years in the bubble of adulthood. She broke off mid-snore and squinted her eyes.

"What's going on? Where are we?" Wylie groggily asked.

She propped herself up and scooted into the other corner of the room. There were only a few feet between them, but Phinn was too afraid to make eye contact. *Focus on her chin*, he told himself.

He started out his explanation with an apology, and swore that he'd tried to keep Olivia occupied as long as possible. He said he was sorry that he screwed up any chance of them getting rescued, but that was also a half-truth. For him, there were too many blank pages that followed an escape from BioLark. He didn't know whether he'd have a place to sleep or if he'd have to call in every last favor to scrape up enough to money for a warm meal. There were homeless shelters he could spend the night in, and plenty of McDonald's Happy Meals in his future, but the rest was uncertain.

Wylie heard him out, but didn't respond. She seemed to prefer to keep silent.

A few hours passed and they didn't say anything to each other. Phinn could hear Wylie's stomach growling, but didn't comment on the familiar sound. He knew it reminded both of them of the mornings they lingered in bed, too lazy to face the rest of the world and eat breakfast.

"How long do you think she's going to keep us in here?" Wylie finally asked.

"I'm not sure. She seemed pretty angry."

"I guess she figured out there were worse ways to torture me than plying me with drugs and conducting experiments on my body. That's all sunshine and roses compared to being trapped in a room with you."

Phinn didn't bother to say he felt the same way. He didn't think it was possible to hate himself more than he did in her presence.

"I never should have brought you to the island," he blurted. "It was wrong to trick you and take you away from your parents."

"Save it, Phinn. I don't want to hear your apologies."

He thought about biting his tongue and turning away from her, but there was more he needed to say.

"What's it like to have a mom and dad who love you?"

The question caught Wylie off guard. He could tell she was debating whether or not to answer.

"I wouldn't know," she finally said. "My parents were a mess."

"Bullshit," Phinn replied.

Parents split up all the time. There was nothing that made the Dalton divorce more extraordinary than what any other broken family had experienced. Phinn wondered what Gregory thought when his kids talked back and stomped up the stairs in the face of the divorce. How hard did he have to bite his tongue so that he wouldn't tell them they were just lucky their parents were still alive and capable of taking care of them?

"It's not bullshit," Wylie mumbled.

Phinn wanted to tell her that her dad would cross oceans and stand up to storms to rescue her. Phinn's parents had never protected him.

"Your parents love you, Wylie," Phinn continued. "It's easier to pretend they don't. You can feel less guilty that way."

"I'd like to point out the hypocrisy of *you* lecturing *me* about guilt and denial."

Wylie pulled herself up from the floor and approached the locked door. She banged her fists on it and screamed at anyone who was listening to let them out. Phinn knew their conversation was probably being listened to or recorded, but that didn't matter to him. Olivia's curiosity would finally be satisfied, too.

"My parents killed themselves," Phinn confessed. "And so did your dad's parents. Same goes for Tinka and Maz."

Wylie turned around and looked at him. "Why are you telling me this?"

"Because it's as much a part of my history as it is yours."

There'd been a time when the Forbidden Side was just another patch of jungle. The plants were lush and overgrown and the pool of water was clear as day. Baby three-legs used to dance around the flowers and burrow into the ground whenever Phinn and the other kids tried to catch them.

"Come on, mommy! Play with me!" Phinn would beg, as he cupped his hand and chased the bugs.

"A little later, Phinny," his mom would respond, barely able to keep her eyelids at attention.

Phinn and the rest of the children had to rely on the teenage natives to keep them company. Lola's family looked far younger than their American moms and dads, but Phinn felt safer with them. He didn't know what was wrong with his parents. He didn't know that the flowers they were eating were making them feel like all was right with the world, as long as they nestled next to each other under the shade of palm trees and uttered random words that never came together in a complete sentence. None of them seemed to need food and they all lost interest in exploring other parts of the island. Before the Forbidden Side was forbidden, it was the only place their parents wanted to be.

"It's dangerous everywhere else," his mom would say to him.

The day they died, Phinn threw a tantrum at breakfast. Lola's parents made him porridge out of boiled chipney and he told them it was disgusting. He threw the wooden bowl into the lagoon and screamed that he wanted Cheerios. And because he was the leader of the pack, Tinka and Maz and Gregory did the same. Meanwhile, Lola happily licked her bowl next to them.

Phinn stormed out of the Clearing where they ate most of their meals, and set off to find his parents in the small enclave they called home.

"They all slept most of the day," he explained to Wylie, "So it wasn't strange to find them lying down with their eyes closed."

He always felt an urge to cry when he remembered the day all of the adults left them. He told Wylie that he'd climbed on top of his mother and begged her to wake up. That he scraped her flesh, hoping the scratches and cuts would summon her from sleep. He even admitted that he rubbed his hands together and placed them on her skin, hoping to warm her up. There were no longer any *rahat* flowers in sight. Their parents had ingested every one. Their hearts simply gave out. It didn't sink in that they were dead until he watched Lola's family dig four graves, for each set of parents who'd overdosed. Tinka was an orphan. Gregory was an orphan. Maz was an orphan. And Phinn promised to take care of them.

Lola's mom and dad told them that what happened was none of their faults.

"The island doesn't take kindly to adults," they'd said.

But Phinn thought they were lying just to make him feel better. He couldn't help thinking if he were cuter or more playful or didn't whine as much, then maybe his parents would have preferred his company to fading away and disappearing completely. He was so engrossed in the memories that he didn't realize that Wylie was quietly weeping.

"My dad had to keep that to himself his whole life," she said, sniffling. "I can't imagine what that must have felt like."

"I can," Phinn said.

"Did you tell me that story to make me feel sorry for you?"

"No," Phinn insisted. "I told you because your dad never had the opportunity to. There were two tragedies that took place the day our parents died. The first was that we grew up without them. The second was that they didn't get to see us grow up."

Wylie cleared her throat and looked him in the eye for the first time.

"Your parents loved you, too, Phinn. Don't you think it was the island that tempted them with *rahat* flowers? It's what happens to adults that live there. They don't survive."

Phinn shrugged. The truth was, they'd never know for certain. Maybe the island didn't see the need to retaliate against unworthy adversaries. It didn't bother to kill people who were already killing themselves.

"Do you know how Olivia found her way back to the island?" Phinn asked.

Wylie shrugged. "She'd probably been searching for it for years."

Phinn shook his head, then told Wylie what he knew from Olivia: that a police sketch of his face had circulated throughout New York City and Gregory had seen it. That years before, Tinka had given Gregory a map to the island, and that he'd purchased a boat and set out to sea to rescue his kids.

"He knew the risks," Phinn said. "He'd heard the rumors that the island wasn't hospitable to adults, but he made the trip anyway."

"What are you trying to tell me, Phinn?"

Phinn didn't tell her that he was trying to right a wrong. He didn't regret taking Wylie and her brothers to the island, but he'd let them believe that their parents wouldn't be completely gutted by their absence. He was scared to touch her, but he placed his hand on her shoulder anyway.

"He's alive, Wylie—don't worry. He was swept up in a storm and nearly drowned, but was rescued by the coast guard. And while he was recovering, he asked Olivia to go find his kids."

"He risked his life for us?" Wylie asked.

Phinn nodded. "He's a good father." With those four words, Phinn felt the hope of redemption. Maybe not in Wylie's eyes, but hopefully in Gregory's.

✦ ✦ ✦ ✦ ✦ ✦

THE TEMPERATURE OF THE BROTH WAS LUKEWARM and the flavor was bitter. Gregory watched as Maura took a bite and politely pretended to like it. He'd forgotten to salt the eggplant and let it soak in cold water before frying it in hot oil, and now the stew was almost inedible. Wylie didn't have much patience as a child, but she never took shortcuts in the kitchen. She had an impressive ability to know when to improvise and when to be methodical. Gregory was a much lazier chef. Just days before she went missing, Wylie and her dad had a huge argument at their neighborhood grocery store after Gregory placed pre-chopped onions in their cart. Wylie had scoffed in disgust and argued that freshly sliced onion was necessary to enhance the flavor of the meal. Anything less than would ruin the integrity of the dish.

"It's so like you to do everything half-assed, Dad."

They both knew she wasn't talking about onions when she mumbled it.

"You don't have to eat it," Gregory told Maura now. "It's not as good as Wylie makes it."

Maura pushed the bowl away. "It reminds me of her," she admitted. "I thought that would feel nice, but it just hurts."

They tried to do things every day that reminded them of their children, but the efforts usually brought them more sadness than comfort. Gregory's recovery was slow and steady, but he was beginning to feel more mobile and less reliant on the pills the doctor had prescribed for the pain. Earlier that day, they'd taken the subway to the East Village to visit Micah's favorite comic book store, and he'd been able to leave his cane at home.

Each morning, he woke up in their living room and told himself that this would be the day that he'd tell Maura everything about Phinn and the island. But by nighttime, he'd lose his nerve. Maura was getting more fragile by the hour and the shock could cause a stroke or a heart attack. He estimated that in a week he'd be able to sail again and would find the island without the help of Olivia. This time, he would make sure to avoid any inclement weather.

"I saw pictures of Abby on prom night again. She posted them to her Instagram for Throwback Thursday," Maura said. Her eyes filled with tears. "She looks so happy with Adam Flanagan. Joshua's only been gone since February. How could she move on so quickly?"

Gregory shrugged, but he knew that teenagers were fickle. He imagined that Joshua's girlfriend had cried her eyes out for the first month that he was gone, but as soon as her friends started debating prom dates and browsing for dresses, she'd been able to carry on. Even Katie Anderson had found a way to move on with her life.

Prior to Gregory's failed attempt at rescuing his kids, he'd learned that Katie had woken up from her coma. At the time, there was no indication of whether she'd suffered permanent memory loss or if she'd be able to walk again. She was awake and that was the most important thing. Gregory was still in need of his cane when he and Maura requested to visit her in the hospital. Her parents stayed in the room the whole time and didn't say much, but at least they allowed them to make the visit. He knew the Anderson family believed that Joshua and his siblings had simply decided to run away so that he could avoid serving time. He wasn't able to tell them about the seventeen-year-old sociopath from his past who'd returned with a vengeance.

Katie was nice to them when she didn't have to be. She said that she hoped their kids would be found safe, and that one day she'd get to meet Joshua so she could forgive him in person. Gregory wanted so badly to tell her that he hadn't raised an entitled brat, and that Joshua was not the type to shirk responsibility. They thanked Katie and her parents, and didn't say a word to each other on the drive home. The Andersons were the lucky ones now. They had their daughter back and she was making great strides. She even insisted on getting out of her hospital bed and hobbling to the door to see them out.

Gregory cleared the table and dumped the rest of the Sweet Honey Stew out in the sink. A dollop of Greek yogurt could have helped cut down the bitterness, but he didn't have the will to try it out. It took him a moment to hear the banging on the door over the wails of the garbage disposal. He turned it off and limped his way to the door.

"Just a minute," he yelled.

Maura came down from the stairs.

"Who is it?" she asked.

Gregory looked through the peephole and found a tear-stained Vanessa standing on their front step, holding a laptop under her arm.

"Mr. Dalton," she said, as soon as he opened the door, "I found Wylie."

✦ ✦ ✦ ✦ ✦ ✦

"SHE POSTED THIS VIDEO AN HOUR AGO," VANESSA said. "I got the notification on my phone, but I couldn't get it to play. I went straight home to watch it on my computer."

Maura squeezed his hand as Wylie's beautiful face filled the screen. She looked tired and scared, but she was alive.

"My name is Wylie Dalton. I went missing from New York City with my brothers several months ago. A woman named Olivia Weckler is keeping us in a facility in upstate New York. I don't know where we are exactly. It was about a three-hour drive from Manhattan. The roads were covered in potholes. We turned left at the train tracks. We walked a mile through the woods across three streams. It smelled like maple or fenugreek. We are in danger. There are fifty other kids—"

The video cut off. Gregory felt his stomach drop. The room was spinning and he needed to take a breath to make sure he wouldn't faint or pass out. He didn't know what any of this meant. Had Phinn originally kidnapped them and taken them to Olivia Weckler? Did that mean his children had never even gone to the island? Or had Olivia lied to him when she claimed she never found the island?

"Olivia Weckler," Maura said. "Isn't that the woman who came to visit you?"

Gregory nodded.

"Call the police," he said.

the missing
dalton kids

no one was coming for them. Wylie's virtual smoke signal hadn't trickled onto anyone's newsfeed. She and Phinn
would die here together. Karma, in its final act, was going
to kill her for every impulsive move and wrong decision.

"How long have we been in here?" she asked.

"Five days," Phinn said.

The hunger and fatigue were starting to seem normal.
Wylie didn't remember what it was like to feel rested and
satiated. Nurse Conway had given them bottled water and a
stack of saltines through a slot in the door, and even though
they'd had the foresight to ration, their stash was down
to one cracker and one bottle of water. At least Wylie was
no longer shaking like she'd just taken part in a polar bear
plunge. There were times she'd wake up drenched in her
own sweat and convinced the crackers were poisoned and
that she was going to die.

"It's just withdrawal." Phinn's teeth chattered as he reassured her. "We've been on a lot of drugs for a long time, and they're finally leaving our system."

He was right. Their bodies were used to taking *parvaz* and *rahat* pills every day. Now that they'd gone without, their organs didn't know how to react. Wylie could handle the chills, but the nausea and cramps made her feel like she was having the most intense menstrual cycle of her life. Luckily, there was a tiny bathroom attached to the room, and when Wylie needed to throw up or just wanted a break from Phinn, she would hide in there until the claustrophobia made her feel even worse.

Phinn didn't bother her much anyway. She wasn't sure if the story about his parents was true or if it was just another case of him manipulating her emotions. If he was being honest, then the story made her feel foolish and guilty. Her childhood was filled with memories of pancakes and Disney movies. It was blissful compared to what Phinn and her dad had gone through.

Wylie had initially tried to ignore Phinn, but chatting with him was the only thing that eased the boredom and quelled her anxiety. Anytime there was a gap in their conversation, she fell victim to intrusive thoughts. She worried that her brothers were being deprived of food for conspiring with Wylie, or that Hopper was getting tortured by orderlies, or that Lola was being treated like a fertility experiment. Her thoughts meandered from her friends to her parents. She wondered if her dad was still recovering from his accident, and whether he'd told her mom the truth about his history. It was possible that Maura had always known about his past, but Wylie had her doubts.

"Sometimes I think your dad's like a complicated algebra problem, and I'll never figure out what X equals," Maura told her once, long before they'd announced their plans to divorce.

Ever since Phinn revealed that her dad nearly drowned trying to get to her and her brothers, she felt a persistent need to see her parents again. Or maybe it was the fever and chills that were making her homesick. She wanted her mom to place her hand on her forehead to check if her temperature was still high and her dad to come home with a giant container of matzo ball soup from the diner around the corner.

"Do you remember your number?" Phinn asked.

"You mean like my phone number?"

"No," Phinn said. "Do you know how many days you have left till you turn eighteen? Have you been keeping track?"

It was hard to delineate the days from each other in this cell. Phinn had brought her to the island on her seventeenth birthday. She'd spent three weeks on Hopper's boat, and twenty-eight days at BioLark. That included the travel time it took them to get to the facility.

"Three hundred and sixteen, I think," she said. "Do you know yours?"

"Somewhere around two hundred and fifty. Not that it matters anymore. I don't have to worry about getting back to the island in time."

"What are you gonna do if we get out of here?" she asked.

Phinn shrugged. "I think I have some family that's still

living. An aunt or two. I could always look them up. I'll figure it out."

He slid the last saltine to Wylie, but she felt bad consuming the entire cracker. She split it in half and shared it with him.

"There's something you need to know about Hopper," Phinn said as he chewed slowly. "You're not gonna like it."

And so it begins, Wylie thought. Phinn couldn't resist. He finally had alone time with Wylie and he was going to take full advantage.

"I don't want to hear any more of your lies, Phinn."

She wished she could go through the rest of her life only being told the truth. She wished that human beings were incapable of lying.

"It's not a lie," Phinn insisted.

"There's nothing you can say that would make me look at him differently. I will never stop being his friend."

"He's only got about three days," Phinn blurted. "That's what you need to know. He's only got about three days until he turns eighteen. I did the math. He'd just turned seventeen when I brought him to the island. He's been in exile for almost a year. I'm only telling you for his sake. Otherwise, he'll lie about it to go back to the island with you, and he'll end up like those other BioLark scientists."

Don't fall for it, Wylie told herself. It was a good lie, but Phinn had a lot of time to come up with it. Hopper wouldn't have kept this from her. He said he was sixteen when Phinn brought him to the island. He would have told her if his time was running out.

"You're making that up to pull us apart."

Phinn shrugged. "Not everything is about you, Wylie. I messed up his life. I'm not going to let him go back to the island just so he can die a horrible death."

Hopper had never told Wylie his number and she'd never thought to ask. They were so caught up in fantasizing about their future on the island that the subject never came up. Maybe it wouldn't be such a bad thing if he celebrated his eighteenth birthday within the confines of a fake jungle. He could have a future with her in New York. Just like the line in Phinn's letter, they could see who they would be ten or twenty years from now. Wylie imagined them debating whether or not to stay in the city or move to the suburbs. She could fall asleep to the sound of his guitar at night, and he could wake up to the sound of her clanking around the kitchen, prepping breakfast.

"Do you love him as much as you loved me?" Phinn asked. "I mean, before we imploded?"

Wylie didn't know if she should give him an honest answer. She didn't want her story to be purely about a girl caught between two guys. Her feelings were none of Phinn's business. He'd lost the privilege of asking questions that dipped below the surface. But before she could open her mouth to tell him exactly that, the lights above them flashed and an alarm blared so loudly that Wylie thought her eardrums had suffered permanent damage.

"What's happening?" she asked frantically.

"I have no idea," Phinn said.

The timbre of his voice shifted. Wylie picked up on an emotion that she'd never detected in the countless times she'd heard him speak: fear. And maybe because she felt the same way, she grabbed his hand and held it tight.

+ + + + + +

SOME OF GREGORY'S FONDEST MEMORIES OF LIFE behind the door of their brownstone took place on summer nights. On the rare evenings when none of his kids made plans with their friends or retreated into their bedrooms to ignore their parents, they would gather in the living room where the cold from the air conditioner blew the strongest. The absence of sun allowed them a break from the heat, but the air was still thick with humidity and sometimes Gregory felt like it was hard to breathe or even speak. It was usually on these nights that he missed the perfect weather on the island. He wished that his past wasn't a secret. He wished that he didn't have to stop himself any time he wanted to describe something as "tropic" or "porcelain." He wanted to turn off the TV, and turn to his wife and his kids and share stories of his childhood and strange upbringing and the reason he still found adults suspect, even though he was one.

He looked at his kids on those nights and wondered which one would thrive in a place like Minor Island. Micah was the one most likely to come out of his shell. He'd probably find a kindred spirit in Tinka. He needed someone who could bust his balls and compliment his artwork at the same time. Joshua would appreciate Phinn's sense of order and the illusion of freedom punctuated by strict rules. Wylie would be the first to fall in love with Minor Island, but she would also be the first to grow bored and restless. It would be the kitchen and vegetables that would suck her in completely—and, of course, the chance to stay seventeen forever. But the magic would wear off. Wylie's personality was too big for deserted islands. She needed to grace the rest of the world with her presence.

"It's cold out here," Maura said.

She was right. The warm Manhattan climate hadn't followed them on the wild goose chase their daughter had sent them on. They'd spent days looking for pot holes and train tracks and wooded areas that smelled like maple. The video that Wylie had streamed on her Facebook page had gone viral, and the police had turned the case over to the FBI. Every news outlet across the country played it on repeat. Now the volunteer center was filled with friends from their neighborhood and Harper Academy, answering the sudden barrage of phone calls. They received hundreds of tips from residents of upstate New York claiming they knew exactly the area that Wylie referenced in her plea for help. But none of them seemed to know the precise location of a secluded building in the woods. There was also no trace of Olivia Weckler. Her family home had been searched, but the Feds didn't find any evidence of fifty kids being kept anywhere nearby. The phone number Gregory had for her was no longer in service. It had only been a few days since Wylie's live stream had hit the internet, but if Olivia knew about it, she'd have enough time to cover up her tracks and come up with a contingency plan.

Gregory took off his sweatshirt and gave it to Maura. He was almost twice her size, and she looked adorable. She placed the hood over her head and it nearly covered her eyes.

"You look like a giant storm cloud," Gregory said.

Maura laughed and held her hands up in the air. "I'm always raining down on you, aren't I?"

There were two FBI agents whose job it was to keep the Daltons out of danger. They forced them to stay a safe distance from the rest of the search party. But after they crossed the third stream and continued the walk through crackling leaves, the excitement was palpable across the vast landscape that divided them from the other agents. They were close. They could all feel it. The scent of maple was so overwhelming that Gregory could practically taste it. He was so proud of Wylie. She'd known to pay attention to her surroundings in case she ever got the chance to send a proper distress signal.

An FBI agent ran toward them. Despite the cold weather, his forehead was sprinkled with beads of sweat and his underarms were soaked from perspiration. He was breathing so hard that Gregory worried he might have a heart attack before he could get his message out.

"We found it," he said. "We found a building. We think this is where your kids are being kept. You need to wait here."

"No," Maura quickly responded. "We need to be there. My husband knows Olivia. He might be able to help."

The exterior of the building took his breath away. It looked like a massive observatory erected in a place with no views. It must have taken years to construct, but Olivia had more than enough funds to put it together. The Feds had the perimeter surrounded, and from where he and Maura were ordered to remain, he couldn't make out any windows or doors. They'd been told to prepare themselves for a stand-off that might last hours or even days.

"We may have to take extreme measures to get your kids home," Agent Sutter explained.

He was the lead agent on the case, and was a man of few words and facial expressions. Gregory regularly caught him rolling his eyes at any mention of magical islands and flowers that could make you fly.

"This is it," Gregory said as he grabbed Maura's hand. "We're going to get our children back."

Maura nodded and squeezed his hand in return.

He didn't want to tell her his next thought. That if their children *had* been to the island, then the versions of them that they'd be getting back would be nothing like the versions that went missing months ago. Those children were gone forever.

"This is the FBI," Agent Sutter shouted into a megaphone, "We'll need your full cooperation."

✦ ✦ ✦ ✦ ✦ ✦

WYLIE HAD TO LET GO OF PHINN'S HAND SO SHE could plug her ears and quiet the sound of the blaring alarm. The flashing lights made her dizzy and reminded her of the migraine spells she sometimes had after her basket-ball games. The rest of the team would go out for pizza, and Wylie would have to go home and crawl under the covers for hours.

"Has this ever happened before?" she screamed at Phinn over the sound of the screeching.

"No," he said.

The longer the alarm sounded, the more terrible outcomes danced around in Wylie's head. The entire building was on fire and they were going to die of smoke inhalation. They were actually closer to the ocean than the woods and the alarm was a tsunami warning. Lola had gone into premature labor and Olivia had triggered the alarm to get the entire staff to assist with the delivery. Bandit had tried to kill himself again, but this time he'd actually succeeded. Whatever amoral tests they were conducting in the labs had been contaminated, and now they were all going to rapidly age until they abruptly died.

Phinn got up and banged on the door. He screamed that they were stuck in here and someone needed to let them out, but Wylie knew no one could hear them.

But then she spotted the knob turning.

Phinn took a step back as the door swung open and nearly hit him square in the face. Nurse Conway stared back at them with his one good eye. He looked disoriented and even paler than normal.

"Olivia needs you," he said.

"What's going on?" Phinn asked.

Nurse Conway grabbed them by the wrist and pulled them out of the room. All this time, his lanky body type fooled Wylie into thinking that he wasn't very strong.

"Your girlfriend is going free."

He led them down the hallway, and Wylie immediately recognized that they were in the same wing as Dr. Jay's hospital room. She hoped he was still alive. Nurse Conway dragged them all the way to the Clearing where the rest of the kids waited. Wylie tried to take inventory of who was present and who was missing. Micah, Joshua, Tinka, and Hopper: present. Maz and Lola: absent.

Her brothers' shoulders sagged with relief when they spotted Nurse Conway yanking her and Phinn toward the group. Olivia stood in front of the crowd. The look of fear and anxiety on her face highlighted her wrinkles, but also made her appear younger at the same time. Her nervous demeanor startled Wylie. She was used to an Olivia who was in complete control of her emotions, however irrational they might be.

Hopper broke off from the group and pulled Wylie into a tight hug. She could see cuts and bruises scattered across his neck, and wondered if he'd resorted to violence to try to find her.

"They found us," he whispered in her ear. "We're going to get out of here. We're gonna get back to the island."

But their joy was cut short by Olivia.

"You did this!" Olivia screamed in Wylie's face. "You broke the cardinal rule! You exposed the island to the world!"

Wylie felt like her head might snap off as Olivia grabbed her by the neck. She could hear the rest of the kids clamoring for Olivia to let her go. Wylie wanted to fight back, but she was weak and tired and was afraid that Olivia would stick her with another needle and put her to sleep. Olivia pushed her face into the lagoon and held it below the surface till Wylie thought she might pass out.

The moment she was pulled out of the water, Wylie could hear Hopper's and Phinn's voices above the rest. They screamed at Olivia to stop, but her loyal army of orderlies restrained them from intervening. Wylie opened her mouth to scream, but Olivia shoved her back into the lagoon and water surged down her throat.

The next time she pulled her up to breathe, Wylie managed to get an arm loose, and elbowed Olivia in the face. Olivia lost her balance and released her grip on Wylie. Blood was dripping down her nose and onto her otherwise pristine lab coat. Wylie wished she'd hit her hard enough to knock her out completely.

"Let them go," Olivia managed to say as she wiped the blood off her face.

"All of them?" Nurse Conway asked.

"No, you idiot. Just Wylie and her brothers. They're the only ones they came for anyway. It's time to admit defeat and head to the safe house."

Olivia looked at their surroundings and shook her head in disbelief. "It'll take years, but I'll build another island."

Wylie sensed a reluctance among Olivia's cohorts. The end had arrived and they would be held accountable. But Olivia was either in denial or just way too stubborn to back down.

"We're not leaving here without our friends," Wylie declared. But before she could give a rousing speech, her throat was inundated with coughs and her eyes stung as they filled with water. Smoke billowed into the room and thickened around them like batter. She didn't know if Olivia was trying to poison them or if the authorities were holding her feet to the fire to set them free. Whatever was happening, it was making her dizzy and nauseous. Hopper held her up, and as she looked at him, she noticed he was completely immune to the smoke.

"It's tear gas," he said.

Wylie felt like her skin was going to bubble and melt until her bones seeped through. She could hear Phinn coughing next to her, and sinking his body into the lagoon for some relief. The nurses and orderlies were doing the same. But none of the other kids seemed remotely bothered by it. And then Wylie remembered they still had *rahat* pills in their systems. Though her vision was beginning to get blurry, Wylie could tell from the silhouette of Olivia's posture that she wasn't feeling the negative impact of the tear gas either. That meant she'd been partaking in *rahat* as well. Aside from the staff, Wylie and Phinn were the only ones who no longer had pain relievers keeping them numb. And yet, somehow through his agony, Phinn's voice emerged above the shouts and residual panic.

"I'll stay with you, Olivia," he said. "You can do whatever you want to me. Just let the others go home. You had a good run, but it's over."

Wylie wasn't at all surprised when Olivia scoffed at Phinn's overture.

"Why would I trust you?" Olivia shouted. "Why would I want to have anything to do with you?"

Wylie was finding it harder to see, but she moved toward Olivia's voice. Even if she went blind, she'd use her other senses to plan her assault. She was close enough now that if she reached out her arm, she'd be able to touch Olivia's neck. *You can do this*, she told herself. *I trust you.*

Wylie jumped onto Olivia's back and grabbed her in a headlock from behind. She heard more yelling, but this time the protests came from adult voices. They'd always outnumbered the BioLark staff, but now the tear gas wouldn't allow the staff to use their Tasers or inject them with sedatives. Wylie coughed from the smoke and fell to the ground on top of Olivia. It felt like her pupils were being bombarded with cataracts, but she felt for Olivia's hair and pulled it tight. She pulled back Olivia's head and pounded it into the ground.

"That's enough, Wylie!" Micah yelled.

Wylie was stronger than she thought. Olivia was no longer moving or fighting back. Through the haze of smoke, she couldn't tell if Olivia was dead or unconscious. At least the *rahat* had prevented her from feeling her skull hit the ground. Phinn snagged Olivia's ID and ripped his mother's necklace off her. Micah searched her pockets and handed a pill bottle to Wylie.

"Take this," Micah ordered. "It's *parvaz*."

Wylie quickly popped the *parvaz* pill and passed the bottle to Phinn. The effects were immediate. As soon as they shot up above the poisoned atmosphere, they were able to see better. The image was one she'd never forget: a mass of teenagers floating in the air while a scattering of white lab coats writhed in pain below them. They were free from their captors, and yet, they still didn't know how the hell to get out of here.

"Go to the deck!" Phinn yelled.

They followed him as he ran down the deck, swinging open the door to each bungalow they passed. Wylie wasn't sure what he was looking for. Maybe he was hoping he'd find Lola and Maz, but none of the rooms were occupied. Finally, he opened one door of a bungalow and let out a yelp.

"Get inside," he ordered.

The bungalow was smaller than most, which meant only a dozen of them could squeeze in at one time. Aside from a chair, there was no furniture inside. Phinn levitated to the ceiling, waved Olivia's ID, and waited for a door to open above them. Phinn pulled a ladder down and directed them to climb up it.

"It leads to the roof," he said. "Go! But don't fly until you know it's safe."

Wylie stood behind him, but she didn't plan to leave. She was only here to make sure her brothers got out in one piece, and then she was going back for the others.

"I'm not leaving Lola and Maz or Dr. Jay," she cried.

"You have to!" Hopper demanded, standing behind her. "I'll get them."

"You'll never make it," she said, suddenly afraid of being separated from him.

"Yes, I will. You have to trust me, Wylie," Hopper said.

She nodded. She did trust him. He wouldn't let her down. Wylie scrambled for the ladder and pulled herself up. Phinn held it steady, allowing her to climb up faster.

The first thing she noticed was that the sky was dark and littered with stars. She could hear a voice echoing through a megaphone, reminding Olivia that they were armed.

The dome-shaped roof blocked Wylie's view of whoever had come to save them. Helicopters paraded overhead and Wylie hoped that none would land on them. Joshua and Micah trickled in behind her. Then Tinka. Then Bailey and Bandit and Nadia and Aldo and Patrick. One by one, they waited until they were together. Wylie kept waiting for Phinn to emerge from the opening next, but he didn't appear.

"He went to help Hopper," Bandit said.

Wylie didn't think Phinn could survive the tear gas again, but she knew it wouldn't do anyone any good if she went back inside.

"Let's fly down," she said. For all they knew, Olivia planned to blow up the building and they needed to get a safe distance away. Wylie floated up in the air and the rest of them followed. They came down the side of the roof and spotted dozens of men and women in suits and bomb squad gear surrounding the building. Wylie watched as their eyes nearly tumbled out at the sight of dozens of teenagers gliding toward them from the sky.

"There's still a few people inside," Wylie called out as she landed on her feet. She heard someone running toward her, but it was too dark to make out the figure.

"*Wylie!*" the person's voice screamed out.

No other voice could make her feel quite as safe or quite as important. It was her mom.

Wylie ran toward her and they embraced.

"Mom," she kept saying over and over again as tears flooded her face.

Behind Maura, Wylie glimpsed her dad walking toward

them as fast as he could. She could tell he was limping.

He looked like the last six months had aged him by years. Dark circles surrounded his eyes, and his formerly dark hair looked frosted over. Micah and Joshua hurried over, and they all threw their arms around each other. It had been six months since they'd been together as a family.

Her parents weren't perfect by any means. They'd made a lot of mistakes, but they didn't deserve to be punished by losing their kids. Wylie felt badly that the other kids didn't have family members here waiting for them, but she knew that in a matter of days, news would spread about the cold cases of missing teenagers who'd been found. She didn't know how anyone planned to get back to the island.

Wylie's own definition of "home" had been lurking in her head for a while, and she could no longer dispute or ignore it. Right now, wrapped in her parents' arms, she knew she was back where she belonged. Some relationships were worth trading eternal youth for.

The reunion was interrupted by a group of EMTs who wanted to check Wylie's and her brothers' vitals. As they took her temperature and measured her blood pressure, she saw that the rest of the kids were being looked after as well. Tinka was nearby, watching Gregory and Maura hover over their kids and ask a bevy of questions of the triage team. Wylie gave her a reassuring smile, and planned to tell her that she was a part of their family now, too.

"Please," Wylie kept saying. "There's more people in the building."

"We've got people looking for them, sweetie," one of the female EMTs replied. "Don't worry."

Just then, a wall in the building burst open, revealing that it had been a hidden door. Wylie saw a hospital bed with a sleeping and oblivious Dr. Jay lying atop of it. It was Hopper who pushed the gurney through the opening.

"We need medical assistance here!" he yelled.

A few more agonizing minutes passed, and then she heard an FBI agent shout that more kids were emerging from the roof. Wylie looked up and saw Phinn and Maz holding Lola in their arms. Wylie broke free of the blood pressure monitor and ran toward her best friend.

Lola coughed from the tear gas and was quickly surrounded by the team of doctors who placed her on a stretcher. Wylie held Lola's hand as they examined her. A doctor placed a stethoscope on her belly, and Wylie stroked Lola's hair to keep her calm.

"I can't feel anything moving," Lola confessed.

The baby was going to survive, Wylie kept telling her. And the child wouldn't be treated like a case study or a lab specimen. The doctor smiled and told them he could hear the heartbeat. They needed to run more tests, but hopefully the baby was okay. Maz was so thankful that he pulled himself onto the gurney and buried his face in Lola's hair. Wylie could see they were crying, and decided to give them their privacy.

A few feet away, Wylie overheard members of the rescue crew trying to process what they'd seen tonight.

"I hope these kids are ready to become famous," she heard one guy say to another. "Their lives are *never* going to be the same again."

Standing nearby, Phinn had heard it too. He looked

at Wylie and she mouthed, "Thank you." Phinn nodded in acknowledgment, but before he could retreat into the crowd, Gregory came barreling toward him.

"You son of a bitch!" Gregory yelled.

Phinn floated up in the air to dodge her dad's punches, while several FBI agents quickly held Gregory back.

"Do you have any idea what you've done to my family?" Gregory continued to shout.

"Dad, please. It's not worth it," Wylie called out. They were all accountable for this mess. No good would come out of attacking Phinn.

Wylie watched as Phinn landed safely on the ground and held up his arms in surrender. It wasn't a fight between equals anymore. Wylie's dad was older and wiser. He'd seen more and lived more. He had a family. Their war was finally over and Gregory had won.

"I'm never going to bother Wylie again," Phinn promised.

The Feds dragged her dad away, and Wylie followed. She stayed with her parents and tried to reassure them that she was okay, but it would take a long time before they were convinced. She hung back to give her brothers a chance to calm their worries.

"We're free," a voice said behind her.

Wylie turned to find Hopper staring back at her. The look of elation on his face told her that Phinn hadn't been lying about his dwindling youth. Hopper's eighteenth birthday was fast approaching and he was thrilled that he'd make it back to the island in time.

"We can go home now," he told Wylie.

She didn't have the heart to tell him that she was already home, but she also couldn't ask him give up his dreams of living on the island to stay with her. It wouldn't have been fair to make him choose after everything he'd already done for her.

"I love you," Wylie said. She'd strung the words together in her head millions of times, but this was the first time she'd said them aloud.

"I love you, too."

She didn't wait to see if he would try to kiss her, since that had gone awry once before. Instead, she placed her hands on his face, stepped up on her toes, and placed her lips on his. For a moment, he stood frozen, and then he kissed her back. It felt different than with Phinn. There wasn't the same intensity or sense of urgency. The kiss with Hopper felt safe and familiar, like it was exactly where Wylie was always supposed to end up, even if she had to take a long and difficult detour to get there.

"Three hundred and sixteen days," was all she could think to whisper in his ear after they broke away from each other. It was a reminder of how much time she had left to change her mind and come find him.

epilogue

rooftops would forever remind him of Wylie. There was no escaping memories of her as he made small talk with adoring strangers and sipped cocktails that weren't strong enough to make him temporarily forget. Tonight should have been about celebrating. Ten months had passed since Wylie sent out her digital flare, got them out of BioLark, and inadvertently catapulted them into the limelight. With most of the other kids back on the island, Phinn was one of the few people left on the mainland to bask in the attention. The footage of them flying out of Olivia's secret lab had dominated the twenty-four hour news cycle. Not only were they teenagers who could fly, but they were teenagers who hadn't aged in years. The entire world was fixated on their story, and fame like theirs would last much longer than fifteen minutes.

Now that Phinn was free to roam the streets, there were girls and boys who threw themselves at him, crazed stalkers who photographed his every move, and producers who bent over backward to work with him. It didn't take him long to have enough money for an apartment in Manhattan that had about as much square footage as a bungalow. He didn't care about hardwood floors or galley kitchens or high ceilings, as long as the place came with a patio. Most nights, he'd drag his pillow and comforter outside to sleep in the cold night air. There was a multitude of city noises that made the natural sounds of the island seem dull and sparse in comparison.

A young girl stared at him from across the rooftop. Phinn smiled at her as she made her way over. He'd been introduced to her before at some other industry party. Phinn knew she was a famous singer-slash-actress, and that she'd been desperate to play Wylie in a movie some high-powered studio executive had put in development. But she didn't look a thing like her. The film's producers assured Phinn they could get her to dye her hair, but he didn't care. She was completely wrong for the part. Pre-production had stalled because they couldn't seem to find anyone young with enough gravitas to play the role of Wylie Dalton.

"Hey, Phinn," she said as she took a sip from her martini.

"Hey . . ." Phinn replied, and clinked his glass against hers. She could keep him company for the remainder of the night, he decided. It was easier to make conversation with one person than deal with tedious small talk with a dozen others.

"Congratulations," she answered. "You were truly a revelation."

Phinn shrugged. "I just get paid to be myself."

"Exactly," she replied with a wide grin on her face.

Phinn had been nervous about the prospect of signing on for a reality show, but he needed the money, and if he was going to be honest with himself, he also craved the attention. The creators had insisted that it wouldn't be salacious or scripted the way other popular shows in the genre had been. Under Phinn's supervision, the series would be tasteful and thought provoking. Phinn was a fascinating figure, they told him, and the country would want to watch him adjust to life after the island. And while Phinn would never admit it, he liked having cameras follow him around. It made him feel less alone. The worst part of his day was when the crew shut down their equipment and left him by himself in his apartment.

"Congrats on the stellar reviews," the girl told him.

Phinn wasn't sure he'd be able to handle it if anyone hated the show, because that would mean they hated him. He kept refreshing Wylie's Snapchat on his phone to see if she'd mentioned the series, but she hadn't posted anything in days. It wasn't like she ever mentioned him anyway. Why would she start now?

"Are you having a good time?" Phinn asked the girl, not sure what else to talk about except for the party.

She nodded, and slipped an olive into her mouth.

"It's a great party. The views are so tropic up here."

Phinn glanced across the rooftop and watched Bandit shake hands and give hugs to more adoring fans. He'd brought his mother to the party. Phinn had been right when he told him that his life was just beginning. Fame and adulthood seemed to agree with him. Phinn spotted Dr. Jay stepping out from the elevator. What happened at BioLark changed his life for the better, too. The public hailed him a hero and a whistleblower, and he went on to release some of BioLark's most groundbreaking work.

Phinn wondered how Olivia felt about Dr. Jay's success. The Feds had searched every inch of BioLark and hadn't found her anywhere. Most of the staff was still serving prison time for holding the kids hostage, but none of them seemed to know what had happened to their fearless leader. The tunnels Dr. Jay had told them about were real, but they'd been found empty and there were no signs of safe houses nearby. Phinn hoped that Olivia had managed to disappear for good and start over. He wanted to hate her, but he'd been the reason for her downfall. Maybe she'd found her way to another island, and was sipping a mai tai and nursing a sunburn while making friends with people her own age.

Phinn knew the polite thing to do would be to walk across the rooftop to say hello to Bandit and Dr. Jay and thank them for coming to his premiere, but it would take him forever to get there with everyone stopping him to chat along the way. He'd already spent an hour or two at the party. No one would blame him for slipping off. He'd known from experience that most true stars never attended their own parties anyway.

"You know, Phinn. I would love to read for the part of Wylie again. I've been rehearsing, and I think I could really hit it out of the park. I could capture her strength and her vulnerability. *All* the things that made you fall in love with her in the first place," the girl exclaimed. "I'd love to have you over to my place one night so we could talk about the script."

Phinn didn't have the energy to fake a polite response. A person like Wylie would never be at a party like this. She much preferred to surround herself with real people.

"I'm sorry," Phinn said to the girl, "But something just came up. I have to go."

He grabbed a pill from his pocket and swallowed it with his drink.

"Do you have an extra one of those?" the girl asked.

Phinn slowly hovered in the air and tossed her a pill. She caught it with one hand and waved good-bye. He was glad she didn't swallow it right away and chase him.

He hadn't planned to fly in the direction of Wylie's brownstone. He'd done everything in his power to avoid her block and her entire neighborhood. Even if it meant that the few cab drivers he had used had to take inconvenient routes to get him from place to place. But tonight of all nights, he needed to get a glimpse of her. He just wanted to make sure she was okay.

On the day they escaped, Wylie had told him she had three hundred and sixteen days to go before she turned eighteen and exactly that much time had passed. Maybe he just wanted to fly past her window to see if her room had been emptied out and she'd returned to the island before her number turned to zero. Maybe he just wanted to wish her a happy birthday, and see if after some distance, they could try to be friends. Despite the way things had ended, Wylie's story would always have Phinn in it and vice versa.

As he soared above Central Park, the people flying past

him pointed excitedly in his direction. Traffic was getting worse and worse these days, and you could never fly with your eyes fixed on your phone anymore. There were too many reports of people crashing into each other, and politicians had proposed laws that would force everyone to wear a helmet while under the influence of *parvaz*. Phinn hoped none of the legislation would pass. It would be a real shame to not feel the wind through your hair while traveling from point A to point B.

He slowly floated to Wylie's fire escape, and quietly landed on the metal railing. The bedroom was dark with only the light from her laptop emanating. There was no one in the room, but the bed looked recently slept in.

Phinn knew she hadn't changed her mind. She hadn't gone back to the island. They were both going to grow old now, even if they'd never grow old together.

"Happy eighteenth birthday, Wylie," he said out loud.

* * * * * * *

THE BOAT INCHED TOWARD THE DOCK AT AN agonizingly slow pace. Wylie didn't have enough patience to wait for it to park, so she started making her way down the deck. For someone whose time was limited, it always felt like Maz took an eternity to get his bearings and greet her. But maybe he wasn't alone this trip.

If Hopper was with him, Wylie told herself, she'd never admit to him or anyone else that she spent some evenings roaming the docks of Jamaica Bay, searching for his boat. It was silly to think he'd tag along today of all days. She was wrong to hope he'd get bored of the island or that he'd realize it wasn't nearly as much fun living there without her. He was probably dating Nadia by now.

But Wylie's heart still constricted when Maz stepped off the boat alone. He gave her an apologetic look, as he carried several boxes in his arms.

"I'm sorry," he said. "It's just me."

Wylie knew it was a mistake to wait for Hopper. Still, she'd come here expecting to see him. After inexplicably making her parents eat pancakes for dinner, she'd gone up to her room and spent a little extra time applying make-up and styling her hair. Her desk was covered with pages from the cookbook she'd devoted most of her free time to. There wasn't much she liked about living in the public eye after the BioLark standoff, but the number of subscribers to her cooking channel had gone through the roof, and had afforded her the opportunity to release a cookbook of Minor Island recipes. It wasn't always easy identifying substitutes for chipney or pame, but Wylie enjoyed the challenge of taste testing recipes and coming up with alternatives.

Thursday nights were reserved for family meals, and her dad would pop over from his apartment with ingredients from his neighborhood garden so he and Wylie could try out her recipes together. That night, he seemed disappointed when she told him that she wasn't in the mood for Sweet Honey Stew, and that she'd preferred her favorite breakfast for dinner. Only Micah knew that her birth date had officially changed. They'd celebrated in February, but since Wylie had stopped aging during the months she'd lived on the island, she was technically still seventeen then. Tonight, when the clock struck midnight, the three hundred and sixteen days she had left after getting out of BioLark would come to an end and she'd officially be an eighteen-year-old.

"Don't be sorry," she told Maz. "It's so good to see you."

A month had passed since his last visit. Wylie helped him place the boxes down and gave him a hug. Sometimes she wished his trips to the mainland were more frequent, and other times she wanted to tell him that she wouldn't meet him on the docks anymore. It hurt too much to be reminded of the island. It was in these moments that Wylie felt empathy for Olivia Weckler. If you allowed yourself to dwell in the past, then life after Minor Island could feel ordinary and dull. They spent the next hour sorting through the boxes. Lola had packed an array of vegetables from the garden and enough sugar roots to last Wylie well beyond the next visit. Wylie had also brought grocery bags of treats and ingredients that were hard to come by across the ocean.

"I threw in some cooking utensils that might make your life easier," she told Maz. He'd been overseeing all of the culinary duties on the island, and needed as much help as he could get.

Maz sent Lola's regrets and promised Wylie that once the responsibilities of motherhood and running the island eased up, she would join him on a trip to the mainland. Before they said good-bye, he handed Wylie a digital camera she'd given him on a previous trip.

"She's growing so fast," Maz said.

The memory card was already filled up with photos of their daughter. They'd named her Almira, after Lola's mom. Wylie grinned as she flipped through the pictures of the baby girl playing in the sand and doing tummy time in the middle of the Clearing. Her favorite photograph was one of Lola holding a beaming Almira while suspended in midair.

"Oh Maz," Wylie said. "She's absolutely beautiful."

There was nothing from Hopper in the boxes. Not a lock of his hair or a handwritten letter or a guitar pick to remember him by. He'd been hurt and blindsided by Wylie's decision to stay on the mainland. At the time, he felt like she was abandoning him. He didn't have a family of his own and couldn't understand why Wylie needed to be with her parents.

"He'll get over it eventually," Maz told her.

"Will you promise to tell him I'm not with Phinn?"

Maz nodded and said he always relayed that message. Wylie thanked him. She didn't want Hopper to ever think that she'd stayed behind to be with someone else. Their conversation turned to Joshua, and Wylie said that her brother was doing as well as could be expected. But she knew that even if juvie was crushing his spirit and making him bitter, Joshua would never admit it. He didn't want his family to worry about him.

"We visited him last weekend. He's got a little over a year to go, and then he'll be home."

It was getting late and Maz needed to run a few errands before making the journey back to the island. She handed him a new memory card for the camera and told him to shower Almira with kisses from her Aunt Wylie. These visits would only last a few more months. Come August, Wylie would be starting her freshman year at UC Berkeley.

She'd chosen the school because of the campus's proximity to Chez Panisse and was determined to snag an apprenticeship in their kitchen. She waited for a few minutes by herself until a car service showed up to take her home. The driver helped her with the boxes, and though Wylie could tell that he recognized her, he didn't ask her any questions about Minor Island. There were stories of teenagers who'd gotten lost searching for the island, but no one from the states or any other part of the world had managed to find it.

"Just Maz again?" Micah asked as he helped Wylie carry the boxes up their stoop.

"Yup," Wylie said.

"We got this in the mail today," Micah said, flashing a postcard at Wylie. She gave the image a closer look, and realized it was a photograph of the Hong Kong skyline.

"Tinka sends her love. She says Hong Kong is her favorite city so far. She hasn't really met too many people yet, but she's content to explore the place by herself."

Wylie would have liked to visit her. They didn't have *parvaz* in other countries yet, and it would be nice to go to a place without hundreds of people flying in the sky. It had taken months for Micah to emerge from his depression after Tinka decided she wanted to travel the world without him, but they were also proud of her for leaving on her own. She used to be the girl who couldn't do anything without a boy at her side, and now she'd used the money she'd earned from an advance on a memoir to get to know the world, and herself, without relying on anyone else.

They carried the boxes through the living room. Ever since they'd gone missing, her mom had instituted a strict eleven-thirty curfew, and Wylie had abided by it. If she were even a minute late, her mom would be on the phone with the police, convinced that Wylie had gone away to Minor Island.

"You're home," Maura said, the relief in her voice obvious.

"Mom. I'm always going to come home. I promise," Wylie replied.

"I'd offer you some dessert," Wylie's dad said, "but you made us have pancakes for dinner, so I don't think more sugar is appropriate."

"Thanks," Wylie said, "But I'm not hungry."

Her parents were sitting on the couch, binge-watching their favorite crime drama. It was one of the many things they'd bonded over the last few months. Wylie knew that geeking out over the same television program wasn't enough to hold their marriage together, but at least it was enough to build a friendship on. And while they were well aware of Phinn's new show—the billboards were hard to miss—they'd agreed not to watch it. Everyone at Harper Academy was planning to tune in, but Wylie didn't need another reminder in her life that he existed.

"I really thought Hopper might show up tonight," Micah said as he climbed onto the fire escape. Wylie handed him a sugar root and followed him out.

"Me too," Wylie said.

The fire escape looked vacant and overly spacious. Joshua's place would always feel empty, and a piece of them would always feel like it was missing until he came home.

"Do you think he's really okay in there?" Micah asked.

"I hope so."

They placed the flame of a lighter under both bulbs of the sugar roots and watched as they melted into a sticky confection. Wylie and Micah waited a few minutes for them to cool off before devouring them. They tried to take small bites and chew slowly to make the treat last as long as possible, but they didn't have the willpower to take their time.

Above them, Wylie could hear the whirr and buzz of New Yorkers flying toward late night adventures. She looked up at the sky, but none of the people soaring in midair were close enough to make out.

Micah glanced at his phone. "It's 12:03," he said, flashing the screen at Wylie. "You are officially an adult. How does it feel?"

"It feels . . . the same," she answered.

They sat on the fire escape together for a few more minutes, but eventually grew tired and said their goodnights. Micah climbed through the window and headed to his room to work on a graphic novel he'd created about Minor Island and BioLark.

The night air was crisp and inviting, and Wylie wanted to enjoy the lack of humidity for a little longer. She was supposed to get up at the crack of dawn to play basketball with Vanessa, but she wasn't ready for sleep. The sounds of improvisational jazz wafted out the window from their neighbor's house, but the notes were too sporadic and seemingly arbitrary to capture her melancholy. She leaned back against the ladder and felt something tickle the nape of her neck. She turned around and the moment her eyes landed on the object, her blood pressure rose. The necklace looked brighter and more polished than the morning after prom when Phinn had given it to her. The chain had been repaired and the glass of the mirror was somehow less tarnished. At first, she was afraid to touch it. She looked around at every corner of the alleyway, but there was no sign of Phinn.

Throw it away, she told herself. *Toss it aside. You don't need it.*

But it was the only souvenir Phinn had left of his mother. It seemed heartless and immature to drop it into some narrow crevice between their brownstone and the one next door.

Wylie unclasped the chain from the ladder and carefully placed it around her neck. It took a few tries to fasten it, but once she did, the charm fell right below her collarbone. She examined her reflection in the mirror, and decided she didn't look a minute older than seventeen. As she grazed the mirror handle with her fingers, she knew she wouldn't take it off any time soon.

It was an artifact of everything she'd gone through. It was a symbol of who she was when she met Phinn, and who she was now. Every time she'd glance at her reflection in the glass, she'd be reminded that the face looking back was the result of her experiences. The good, the bad, the ones that made you grow up a little faster than you wanted. Most of all, it would remind her of first loves. And last loves. And everything in between.

"Good-bye, Phinn," she whispered.

And then she climbed into her bedroom and closed the window shut. It was quiet in their house. Joshua wasn't in the next room listening to his favorite presidential speeches at top volume. Micah wasn't drowning his sorrows in a bottle of Jameson and yelling at Joshua to turn his speakers down. No one was getting belligerent downstairs or trading marital barbs. And Wylie wasn't tossing and turning from the fear of getting older. Tonight, her first night as an adult, she would fall asleep just fine to the silence.

ACKNOWLEDGMENTS

Some authors describe writing as a lonely endeavor, but I had the opposite experience with this book. It came together with the support and help of so many.

To Kendra Levin—I am so lucky that I got to work with you on not one, but two books. You went above and beyond as my editor, and these characters would not be as fully formed without your guidance, thoughtfulness, and storytelling expertise. Thank you so much for challenging me and making me a better writer. I will forever be spoiled from working with you.

Thank you to my agent, Jess Regel at Foundry Literary + Media. What started out as a few chapters turned into two books, and that is in large part due to your superhuman efforts and tireless work. Partnering with you was a turning point in my career, and remains one of the best decisions I've ever made.

I was very fortunate to work with the talented team at Viking Children's Books, who helped bring both *Never Ever* and *The Lost Kids* to life. To Dana Li, the creative mind behind the stunning covers, I'm more than happy to have each book judged by them. To Kate Renner, for her beautiful interior designs: you took boring Word documents and made them sparkle. To Janet Pascal, Marinda Valenti, and Debra DeFord-Minerva for every single copyedit, and for bearing with me through many a typo. Thank you as well to Maggie Rosenthal for all of your help and assistance these last few years.

Thank you to Tom Jacobson, Blye Faust, and Wendy Rhoads, who were early advocates of this story when it was just a one-liner in my head. *The Lost Kids* would not have happened without *Never Ever*, and I would not have attempted to write either book without your encouragement.

To Lynn Fimberg, David Rubin, Michael Pelmont, Matt Ochacher, and Eric Brooks, for always being a phone call away. I would be in a constant state of indecisiveness without your advice.

To Samira Saedi Abrams and Kia Saedi—if an evil doctor ever held you against your will, I would totally find a way to save you. That's just the kind of thing that siblings do for each other. Thank you for providing me with a surplus of happy childhood memories, and for being the inspiration behind these books. And to Jacob Abrams (my brother from another mother), for opening the very first door in my writing career.

A very special thank-you to my parents, Ali and Shohreh Saedi, for teaching me the meaning of perseverance. I would not have had the courage to pursue my dreams if I hadn't been raised by people who believed in me. Not to mention all those weekends you drove four hundred miles to take care of your grandson so I could meet my deadlines.

To my amazing husband, Bryon Schafer. You make me feel like I can do anything. Thank you for being a sounding board whenever I needed one, and for having all the confidence in the world in me. You are a bright light and I love you so much.

And to little Ellis, for upping your nap game so I had time to finish this book. Who needs pixie dust when they have you? Thank you for giving me my biggest adventure yet. I love you.